CHAPTER 1

'Is he dead?' Dalton asked.

Loren Steele waded for another pace into the river, then prodded the floating body with a stick.

'I reckon so,' he said, 'but help me get him to the side.'

Dalton joined Loren in the water and, with Loren taking one arm and with Dalton taking the other, they dragged the limp body out of the water and deposited it on the riverside. When they turned the body over Dalton saw that the face was that of a young man and that he still had a healthy complexion, suggesting this unfortunate person hadn't been in the water for long. But when he felt for a pulse the skin was cold.

A search of his pockets didn't reveal any details of who this person was. Although both men saw the charred hole in the man's jacket which, when they lifted the jacket, covered a darkened patch of his vest.

'Gunfights are common up in Durando I hear,'

Dalton said.

'They are, but he couldn't have come from there. He hasn't been in the water for more than a few hours.'

Dalton considered the body and noticed the motif stitched into the breast of the man's jacket.

'The letters D, M and C,' he said, squinting as he discerned the ornately written legend. 'Durando . . . Mining Company?'

Loren nodded. 'Then that's worrying. Our town doesn't need trouble from Durando getting closer. I wonder how close it came this time?'

'There's only way to find out.' Dalton pointed towards town. 'But we'd better check with Wes first.'

As one of Two Forks's original settlers Wes Potter had unofficially assumed a position of authority and on most matters everyone requested his opinion. So they returned to Loren's house to collect his wagon; then, after they'd loaded the body on to the back of the wagon, they headed into town.

As expected they gathered interest without requesting it and so when they drew up outside Wes Potter's barn, they had collected a trailing group of concerned-looking townsfolk.

Wes shooed them away to avoid an unseemly scene developing. Everyone was slow to respond, but after looking at the body and registering their disgust and respects most people went away, leaving just several men along with Dalton's wife, Eliza.

'We'll give this unfortunate man a decent burial,' Wes said after a short consideration. 'And we should

Dalton's Mission

When Dalton and Loren Steele happen across an ambushed gold shipment, they are too late to help. Everyone dies, attackers and defenders alike. Being honest men they try to return the gold to Perry Haynes of the Durando Mining Company, its rightful owner, but unbeknown to them Perry has been overthrown.

With corruption and the law of the gun now ruling in Durando they are slammed into jail on the dubious charge of having stolen the very gold they had rescued!

The two men befriend Perry but to help him reclaim his mine, they'll have to strap on their six-shooters and tame the hell-hole that is Durando.

Dalton's Mission

Ed Law

A Black Horse Western

ROBERT HALE · LONDON

© Ed Law 2009
First published in Great Britain 2009

ISBN 978-0-7090-8833-2

Robert Hale Limited
Clerkenwell House
Clerkenwell Green
London EC1R 0HT

www.halebooks.com

Typeset by
Derek Doyle & Associates, Shaw Heath
Printed and bound in Great Britain by
CPI Antony Rowe, Chippenham and Eastbourne

note that his is the first body that's drifted downriver, but it won't be the last.'

'But the problem is,' Dalton said, 'he didn't die in Durando.'

Wes sighed. 'The nearest law is Sheriff Blake in White Falls and he's more than a week away.'

'Which is why we can't leave it to Blake.'

Wes looked at Loren, who nodded, so they knocked the subject back and forth until they reached an agreement. It was a decision that one person didn't like.

'I don't want you to leave,' Eliza said, concern watering her eyes. 'Just because there's trouble, it doesn't mean you have to sort it out.'

'I'm going with Loren and Wes,' Dalton said. 'We won't be gone for long and if we can find out anything about where that man came from, it'll put all our minds at rest.'

'Mine won't be at rest for every moment you're away,' she murmured before she gave him a brief hug and backed away, avoiding making this any harder for him.

Dalton gave her a nod and a smile that said he'd be back soon. Then, while he and Wes got their horses ready and Loren jumped back on to his wagon, the townsfolk who had stayed to discuss the matter dispersed.

Only one man remained, watching them silently. This man had joined the settlement only recently and Dalton had yet to speak with him, knowing only that his name was Kyle Mallory.

7

'You got anything to say about this, Kyle?' he asked.

'Yeah,' Kyle said, casting furtive glances at the body. 'I'll come with you. I know the area upriver.'

'So do I,' Loren said, leaning forward in his seat to look at Kyle. 'I've hunted upriver for over two years. I know every tree and every trail up there.'

'Except I'm guessing you stayed nearer to Two Forks than Durando. I passed through Durando a month ago.' Kyle shrugged when nobody responded. 'And besides, since I arrived I haven't been much use. This'll give me a chance to get involved in town business.'

This comment removed everyone's doubts and so with a series of grunts it was agreed that the newcomer should join them.

Fifteen minutes later the four men headed out of town to go upriver, but they travelled in pensive silence. Each man was lost in his own thoughts about what they might find ahead while searching the riverbanks for clues as to where this man had died.

They became more animated when they reached a sharp rise where the river had formed a waterfall. They dismounted to help Loren manoeuvre the wagon on to level ground. Then they rested awhile and each man couldn't help but look down into the valley.

The distant town of Two Forks was still visible, this being the last time they'd see it until they had completed their mission, and from here it was clear why the townsfolk had so named the settlement.

The peaceful town stood at the meeting point of three rivers, a location that had created a fertile and inviting stretch of land. In the four years since the first settlers had arrived Two Forks had grown to provide a home for thirty families and few months passed without more people arriving.

Each family had been attracted by the abundant food from the river, the ease of growing crops and the hunting. But Two Forks wasn't growing as quickly as the town situated several days upriver was. Worse, in Durando the attraction to settlers was baser: gold.

Ever since prospectors had ridden into White Falls, the largest town in the area, with tales of lucky strikes, people had swarmed there. Quickly they had created a hell-hole of lawlessness and depravity that everyone in Two Forks hoped would never affect them.

Last year Dalton had found a small nugget of gold that had washed downriver and others often idly searched the water for more nuggets, but never seriously. Everyone in town had something that was more important. They had a community, and for that reason as much as anything else, the four men who turned their backs on their home and headed higher into the hills hoped to return to that life as soon as possible.

They'd been riding for another hour with Kyle bringing up the rear and with Wes scouting along ahead when Wes came riding back through a dense thicket. Before he had even opened his mouth Dalton could see from his stern expression that he had bad news.

'I've found where our body came from,' he said with a pronounced gulp. 'And he wasn't the only one to die.'

With Wes's statement preparing everyone for the worst, the group headed on, working their way through the thicket. When they emerged before them lay the aftermath of a pitched and bloody battle.

A wagon lay on its side beside the water. Its unbroken wheels and cargo of three crates lying on their sides suggested it'd been tipped over. Two horses lay dead. One man dangled from a wheel, his chest bloodied, a raised and twisted arm trapped in the wheel keeping him upright.

Another man lay beside the wagon, face down, while another man lay half-in the water. The current made his arms wave as he waited for the water level to rise a few inches so that he could join the other man in a final journey downriver.

'Wes, Kyle,' Dalton said, 'scout around. We'll check on these bodies.'

Although everyone accepted Wes as being in authority while in town, out here he was happy to defer to Dalton, so all three men nodded. Wes and Kyle looked around, picking where they'd explore first, while Dalton and Loren jumped down and paced towards the wagon.

They were ten yards away when a gunshot rang out.

All four men froze then jerked around, looking

for where the firing had come from, but when a second shot ripped out, Dalton saw splinters kick off the side of the wagon. That told him everything he needed to know.

'Get behind the wagon!' he shouted.

He hurried to the wagon and hunkered down at the side, then drew his six-shooter while beckoning for the others to follow him into safety. No other shooting sounded as the three men ran towards him and he couldn't see where the shots had come from.

He slapped each man on the back as they hurried into hiding before joining them. Then he jerked backwards in surprise when he saw that the scene behind the wagon was as bad as that in the open space with three more bloodstained bodies lying on their backs. Each man had the same motif on his jacket of 'DMC' as the man they'd fished out of the river had.

More rapid gunshots rang out, the first two tearing into the top of the wagon and spraying splinters down on them. The next volley ripped into the sides of the wagon, the shots being almost simultaneous and proving that there was more than one person out there.

'They're keeping us pinned down,' Kyle grumbled.

'Or they're keeping these men pinned down,' Loren said as he knelt beside the first man. 'They're still alive, or at least this one is.'

This comment made Wes join Loren. He had some medical knowledge and he reported that this man, although wounded, would live. Of the other two men, both had been holed repeatedly and were dead, but when Wes prodded the wounded man he murmured in pain, then opened his bloodshot and tired eyes.

'Did Billy get word to you?' he asked after murmuring that he was Dan Clarke. 'He was the youngest so I sent him away.'

'In a way he did,' Dalton said using a grave tone that made Dan wince. 'We're from Two Forks.'

'Then I'm real sorry I got you involved. Go. This ain't your battle.'

'It wasn't, but that changed when we got shot at.'

'I ain't sure about that,' Loren said from behind him. 'We were out in the open, but the shooting was at the wagon. They could have picked us off easily if they'd wanted to.'

'Perhaps they could have, but we ain't leaving this man to die and neither can we leave with him and not get fired at.'

'Then what can we do?'

To avoid answering that he didn't know Dalton edged to the side of the wagon and risked glancing out to consider the situation. The land sloped upwards gently from the river presenting plenty of cover for the men who were keeping them pinned down.

He was searching for the most promising-looking escape route when a bullet whined past him and scythed into the river, making him leap into hiding behind the wagon. He dragged his jacket round to look at the cloth.

'You hit?' Loren asked.

'No, but that was mighty close. And I reckon that means whether we want it or not, this is now our battle.'

His colleagues grunted that they agreed and with that matter concluded they hunkered down. They questioned Dan as to why he was fighting for his life. Despite their help, he remained tight-lipped, so Dalton looked around the side of the wagon again.

Two men were working their way towards the wagon. They were running hunched over, aiming to come at them from both sides, but on seeing Dalton they both swung their guns up and fired.

Dalton jerked back out of view as one bullet tore into the base of the wagon and the other sent a wheel spinning.

'This is serious,' Kyle murmured unhappily. 'How many are out there?'

This time Dan did provide an answer.

'I reckon,' he said, 'we'd cut their numbers down to two before they got the last of us.'

This information was all Dalton needed to hear. He gestured to Loren that he should take up a position on the other side of the wagon. Loren nodded and moved off. Then on the count of three both men raised themselves and risked moving out from their cover to fire at the approaching men, but they had gone to ground.

Dalton fired only once before stilling his trigger finger, then darted back. He glanced at Loren who grunted confirmation that he couldn't see where the men were hiding either.

Then the shooting started.

Rapid gunfire slammed into the wagon, the slugs coming from close to and aimed low. After a few shots lengths of the wooden base of the wagon splintered and fell away, meaning the cover they had wouldn't remain effective for much longer.

So Dalton braced himself, then leapt away from their rapidly holing cover, firing wildly as he ran. Then he dived. He hit the ground, rolled over a shoulder and came to rest on his belly, looking away from the river.

This new position let him see that the two men were hunkered down in a hollow twenty feet from the wagon. One of them had followed his progress and his gun was arcing round to aim at him. But Dalton was quicker.

His high shot to the man's chest sent him reeling. Quickly he planted a second bullet in his side before the man hit the ground.

Then Dalton pressed himself to the earth, presenting a small profile while he reloaded. With quick actions he thrust bullets into the chambers, then swung the gun up, but it was to look down the barrel of the second man's gun.

Before Dalton could shoot, gunfire roared. To his relief the man staggered back a pace, clutching a wounded shoulder. The man righted himself and blasted off a round at the wagon. By then Dalton had him in his sights and tore off two quick shots that sent him spinning away to land on his back.

For several seconds Dalton stayed down to ensure nobody else made their presence known. Then he got to his feet and, doubled over, ran back to the wagon where he found that his saviour wasn't the man whom he'd expected to have fired.

Dan, the last survivor from this stand-off, had shot the man, but he had paid for his bravery with a returned bullet to the neck.

Wes couldn't help him. Without uttering another word he died.

There was nothing for the rest of them to do but to confirm that no other men had survived this pitched battle. So, while Kyle and Wes checked close to the wagon, Loren and Dalton scouted around.

They soon found where their assailants had first ambushed the wagon when they came across three bodies a way up the slope at a position where they had been able to look down on the wagon.

'At least twelve dead men,' Dalton said, tipping back his hat as he surveyed the sorry scene. 'I wonder what they were fighting about?'

'No idea,' Loren said. 'But let's hope whatever it was ended when the last of them bit the dirt.'

Dalton murmured that he agreed with this sentiment. Then, in a sombre state of mind, they made their way back down to the wagon. By the time they reached the river Kyle and Wes had righted the wagon and declared it fit for travel.

'Why bother?' Dalton asked. 'This wagon is so full of holes it ain't no use to anyone.'

'We need one for the bodies,' Kyle said. 'And one for the cargo the wagon was carrying.'

'I ain't so sure about that,' Wes said. 'The cargo ain't ours.'

Kyle opened his mouth to argue but Dalton butted in before he could comment.

'What cargo?' he asked.

'While you were gone,' Wes said, pointing at the three crates he and Kyle had lined up, 'we've found the reason why all these men died.'

'Which is?' Dalton asked. He paced over to the wagon, but Kyle and Wes didn't answer other than to give low whistles. When Dalton looked in the nearest crate, he produced a low whistle himself.

The crate was filled to the brim with shining gold.

CHAPTER 2

'So,' Kyle said with awe in his tone as he joined Dalton in peering into the crate, 'here's the reason why men go to Durando.'

'And why men die,' Dalton murmured. He hunkered down beside the crate and although the sight didn't impress him, he still felt a need to reach in and pull out a handful of the contents.

The gold hadn't been refined, many nuggets being encased in rock, but there still had to be many pounds of precious metal in each crate, and he didn't like to think how much it was all worth. The other men didn't know either, but they did know one thing for sure.

'We have to get away from here,' Wes said to a chorus of approval. 'Presumably Dan and these men were taking a gold shipment away from Durando, but if this many men were prepared to die to get their hands on it, there could be more of them out there.'

'Yeah,' Loren said. 'We've learnt enough here. We'll give the bodies a decent burial in Two Forks,

17

but aside from that, this ain't got nothing to do with us.'

Dalton grunted that he agreed, and they moved off to begin loading the bodies on to the back of their wagon. Kyle didn't join them.

'What about the gold?' he asked. 'We can't just leave it here.'

'Can't see why not,' Dalton said, shrugging before he helped Loren lift the first dead man.

Kyle waved his arms as he struggled to voice his reasons why this was a bad idea, giving Wes enough time to drag another body closer and for Dalton and Loren to load it on the wagon.

'Because,' he said, finding his voice at last, 'someone might come along and steal it.'

Despite the grimness of the carnage around them, this made the other three men laugh.

'Anyone can come along and steal all they like,' Dalton said, still chuckling. 'As Loren said, this ain't our business.'

'But it sure is the business of whoever's gold this really is. I know if it were mine, I wouldn't be pleased if some people left it out here in the open for anyone to happen across.'

'I can see your point,' Dalton said, looking around with his eyebrows raised, inviting opinions. 'Perhaps we can't just leave it here.'

'It's a long way up to Durando,' Wes said, 'if you're minded to find its rightful owner.'

'It is,' Loren said. 'So we could keep it safe in Two Forks until someone comes along and claims it.'

18

Dalton gave a significant look at the bodies before he replied.

'That's inviting trouble our way that Two Forks doesn't need, and besides, how will we judge who is the rightful owner?'

Loren lowered his head and murmured that he didn't know. So the four men stood in silence with nobody offering any other suggestions until Kyle spoke up, using a light and joking tone.

'Who's to say we have to hand this gold over to anyone?' he asked.

'You can't be serious,' Dalton muttered.

'Sure. We could take it back to Two Forks and bury it, and then. . . .' Kyle removed his hat and slapped it against his thigh, grinning. 'You Two Forks folk sure are easy to fool. I was joking.'

Everyone uttered a snort of laughter while Kyle continued to grin.

'I reckon,' Dalton said, still eyeing Kyle and wondering whether his comment had been a joke, 'unless anyone has a better idea, we should take this gold back to Durando, after all. We'll take the bodies too and leave them at this DMC, then let them sort out the rights of what happened.'

'And,' Loren said, 'if we meet anyone else who wants this gold as desperately as these men did?'

'They can have it.'

Wes and Loren grunted that they agreed, but Kyle was still smirking after his earlier joke and didn't change his expression.

*

19

'You reckon we can get there before noon?' Dalton asked.

'Yeah,' Kyle said from the other wagon. 'It's ten miles on, so we should be heading back to Two Forks today. And it sure couldn't come soon enough. This stink ain't doing me no good.'

Dalton smiled sympathetically, and for the second time today they swapped wagons. He took control of the wagon carrying the bodies while Kyle climbed on to the wagon carrying the crates of gold. Loren continued to ride along on his own.

Despite everyone's misgivings the journey from the scene of the ambush had passed without incident. In fact their passage had been so peaceful that after the first day Wes had returned to Two Forks to let the townsfolk know what had happened while the other three men had continued on to Durando.

Dalton had avoided thinking about what his wife would think of this extension to their mission. But he had consoled himself with the thought that it would be a quick journey, as they'd found enough provisions on the ambushed men to let them ride without wasting time foraging.

So with nothing else to distract them they'd kept a close eye on their surrounding and someone had stood guard throughout the night. But they'd seen nothing untoward.

With the long summer days and dry weather they'd converted what could be a two-week journey in mid-winter into a three-day trek. They'd ridden along beside the river and seen the broad and languid-flowing water that passed by Two Forks gradually convert itself into a foamy and fast-flowing river that hurtled through deeply gorged passes.

Despite their speed Dalton and Loren weren't looking forward to their first visit to Durando. Kyle hadn't been as forthcoming as he'd promised about what they would find there other than to tell them that it had taken him only an hour to decide the place wasn't for him. Luckily he'd taken the same amount of time to decide Two Forks was the right place for him.

From the little he had learned during his short stay he'd discovered that the Durando Mining Company was five miles out of Durando. So they all hoped they would be able to complete their mission without the necessity of entering the town.

The mine was run by Perry Haynes and Kyle had heard he was an honourable businessman. So feeling as optimistic as they could be in the circumstances, they rested awhile in a clearing to water their horses and discuss the story they would relate when they arrived.

Loren agreed to Dalton's suggestion that they shouldn't mention they had helped fight off the raiders but Kyle didn't join in their deliberation. Instead he paced nervously back and forth before disappearing into the bushes for so long that Dalton and Loren exchanged amused glances.

When he did eventually emerge, rubbing his stomach ruefully, he ignored their ribbing about the effect of his nerves on his constitution and climbed on to the wagon that was carrying the gold, even though it wasn't his turn. Neither Dalton nor Loren complained as they set off at a good pace, now keen to finish the task quickly and embark on the journey home.

Using Kyle's directions they veered away from the river. When they'd emerged from the tree line they were in a winding boulder-strewn pass. Gradually the terrain became starker and from ahead the sounds of industry grew. When they passed over a ridge they saw ahead of them the entrance to the gold mine, as Kyle had promised.

Milling over a craggy hill were dozens of scurrying figures. The hill itself was pitted and holed. A high ridge surrounded the hill, providing a natural barrier to would-be entrants, and forcing anyone approaching to head through the pass. Accordingly this ridge had been blasted through to provide an entrance to the mine. On either side of the entrance two men with rifles stood sentinel, watching their progress.

With Kyle struggling to get the gold-laden wagon up the last length of slope, Dalton hurried his own lighter wagon on ahead with Loren at his side.

'We've got a delivery for Perry Haynes,' he shouted as he approached.

This comment made the two guards look at each other.

'Perry?' one man asked.

'Yeah. We've been told he runs the Durando Mining Company.'

The two men glanced at each other again. Then one man made his way towards the wagon while the second stayed back, viewing them with suspicion. When the guard came close enough for him to see the bodies in the back of the wagon his own suspicion made him raise his rifle and aim it at Dalton.

'That's close enough,' he hollered. 'Your first wrong move will be your last.'

Dalton drew the wagon to a halt then raised his hands from the reins. 'We don't want no trouble. We're just bringing these men back here for you to sort this out.'

The nearest guard paced around to the side of the wagon and looked in. The sight made him raise his eyebrows, He turned to Dalton.

'You claiming you had nothing to do with this?'

'If we had, do you think we'd be foolish enough to come here?' Dalton waited for the guard to provide a non-committal shrug. 'We came across the aftermath of a pitched battle downriver. From the letters on the jackets we reckoned they were your men.'

The guard rubbed his chin as he pondered this. Dalton caught Loren's eye and they exchanged glances.

'You'd better come on in and tell your story to Cornelius.' He pointed at the approaching Kyle, then at the other guard. 'You two stay here.'

'We'd prefer to see the mine owner, Perry Haynes.'

The guard shook his head. 'The likes of you will only get to see Cornelius.'

With that surly comment he gestured ahead for Dalton and Loren to enter the mine encampment. At a slow pace they trundled through the entrance to come out on to a wide flat area.

The hill was to their right. To their left was a group of around fifty grimy tents. Some miners had even made homes in the open, beneath overhanging stretches of the ridge. Over the whole area there was a pall of smoke, the stench of uncared for humanity, and a continuous susurration of industrial noise.

In response to the guard's instructions they headed for a large blasted-out opening in the side of the hill, where around a dozen men had congregated.

Their slow progress attracted interest, so by the time Dalton stopped before the opening ten men had left the encampment to flank him. They all peered at the bodies while murmuring to each other. All were dirty, their clothes and skin coated with baked-on dirt so that only their eyes betrayed their feelings, and in Dalton's view they were merely of idle curiosity.

Two men made their way down towards them, these men being cleaner than most of the others here were. They talked with the guard and Dalton overheard that they were the overseer Cornelius Gash and Brady Cox, presumably Cornelius's second-in-command. Then Cornelius demanded to hear Dalton's story.

Dalton judged Cornelius to be authoritative enough to make him the only person they'd need to talk to, so he related the version of events they'd agreed earlier. He didn't mention that they were from Two Forks, instead telling him a tale of their moving upriver while hunting and coming across the bodies. As they were heading towards Durando anyhow, they had decided to bring them here.

'You looking for a reward?' Cornelius grunted when he'd finished.

Dalton shrugged. 'Being grateful is your concern, but we saw what was in the crates. It sure looked like a lot of gold to me.'

The mention of the gold removed some of the truculence from Cornelius's attitude.

'You brought that back too!' he murmured, sounding genuinely surprised, then looked around. 'Where is it?'

'Back at the entrance.'

Cornelius gestured to Brady, who quickly hurried to a horse, then, with the guard, galloped off to fetch Kyle.

'Maybe I misjudged you. I don't exactly get to meet many honest men up here, so I'm obliged you brought the gold back.'

Dalton smiled. 'Being obliged is all we asked for. If you get someone to take the bodies, we'll be on our way.'

'Sure,' Cornelius said. Then he barked orders to the milling miners to unload the wagon.

While they worked Dalton kept his gaze set

forward to avoid seeing what, from the grumbles he heard, was clearly an unpleasant task, but then a warning cry from behind made him turn.

Brady was galloping back towards them from the entrance waving his rifle over his head.

'Cornelius,' he shouted when he came closer, 'we've got trouble. The gold has gone!'

CHAPTER 3

'Gone?' Cornelius murmured.

'Yeah,' Brady said as he drew his horse to a halt. 'Rory is lying on the ground knocked out and the other wagon ain't around no more.'

'I knew it was a trick.' Cornelius swirled round to confront Dalton.

'It wasn't,' Dalton said raising his hands slightly. 'There's got be a mistake.'

Cornelius glared at him, his firm jaw conveying his contempt. Then he delivered a few grunted orders that encouraged several men from around the main opening to the mine encampment to join him.

Dalton noted that, like Cornelius, these men were cleaner than the rest. He also noted that Loren was looking at him and shaking his head, his forlorn expression showing that he didn't think there had been a mistake.

Dalton lowered his head, accepting that he was probably right. Kyle was a recent arrival in Two Forks and he'd yet to get to know him well. He'd also been the one who had suggested keeping the gold, although at the time Dalton had decided it was a joke.

Dalton and Loren kept quiet when Cornelius ordered them down from their horses. Standing together they watched the men get ready for their pursuit of Kyle. When Brady had received his final instructions and was ready to leave, Cornelius gestured up the hill to a point about fifty yards from the encampment opening.

'Get over there,' he said, pointing.

They set off towards the hill with Cornelius following, but when they'd made their way up the slope for about thirty yards Dalton saw where he was directing them and he stopped.

Ahead was a small cave. Although it appeared to be natural in origin, unlike many of the holes bored into the hill, rusted iron bars had been made into a gate and set across the entrance. The presence of a man standing guard at the entrance suggested this was a rudimentary jail.

'You've got no reason to put us in there,' Dalton said. 'We didn't know Kyle would take the gold.'

'Maybe you did, maybe you didn't.' Cornelius pushed Dalton towards the cave. 'But you'll stay in there until I have the gold back and I get to the truth.'

Dalton dug his heels in to stop himself, then turned.

'We did you a great service. If we'd have wanted to steal the gold, we'd have just taken it instead of coming here.'

Cornelius's slight narrowing of the eyes suggested that he did understand it was unlikely that they had planned this, but he still pointed at the cave.

'Be quiet!' he demanded. 'And get in there.'

The guard moved in and slapped a hand on Dalton's shoulder. Dalton threw the hand away and looked around, weighing up their chances. The bulk of Cornelius's men were riding towards the entrance and the rest of the miners weren't paying this confrontation any attention.

If they could reach their horses, they might be able to escape, but that would only encourage the belief that they were guilty.

'All right,' he said, spreading his hands in a show of resignation, 'we won't resist, but instead of locking us up, let us help you get the gold back before that double-crossing Kyle gets too far away.'

Cornelius sneered as the guard frisked, then disarmed Dalton, but when he saw that he didn't resist, he turned to wave towards the entrance.

'Brady,' he shouted, 'get back here. You're getting some help.'

'Obliged,' Dalton said.

'You certainly will oblige.' Cornelius gestured for the guard to seize Loren. 'Because while your friend enjoys our hospitality only you are going after the gold. If you don't get it back, he won't enjoy that hospitality for long.'

'You don't know where Kyle's gone, do you?' Brady Cox said, not for the first time, except this time

Dalton was also wondering whether that was the case.

The pass was the only route away from the mine and after confirming that Kyle hadn't gone to ground amongst the short gullies and ravines nearby they'd headed towards the river.

Now, half an hour after they'd entered the tree line Dalton faced his first decision. The trail split into two, one route being a grassy and rarely used path down to Two Forks beside the river, the other being the well-used trail that veered away from the river and headed towards Durando itself.

'I don't know nothing for sure,' Dalton said, 'but I do know Kyle didn't like what he saw in Durando. He wouldn't go there again.'

'Then he ain't no fool.' Brady considered the well-worn path, then shrugged and moved on towards the river. 'But you'd better hope you're right.'

Dalton said nothing as he filed in behind Brady in the middle of the group of six riders. As they rode on he leaned from the saddle, but he couldn't pick out any wheel ruts either from their journey upriver earlier or from Kyle's escape.

There were several vantage points where they were treated to a panoramic view of the river. At each one they stopped and everyone peered downriver, searching for tell-tale movement, but each time they saw nothing.

As they closed on the clearing where earlier the three men had rested awhile before embarking on the final leg of their journey, his colleagues were becoming restless and were muttering in an irritated manner.

Dalton reckoned he wouldn't be consulted for much longer, so he thought through everything he could remember about Kyle, hoping to recall something that would aid him. But he knew little about him and could think of no new ideas.

'This is far enough,' Brady said as they arrived in the clearing. 'We ain't following your lead and letting your friend get further away. We head to Durando. Someone will have seen him there.'

Nobody looked at Dalton to see what his opinion was, neither did he feel inclined to voice one. He did feel as if he'd led Brady on a pointless detour based on his belief that Kyle would return to Two Forks.

Then he remembered something about Kyle.

'Wait,' he called out. Nobody listened to him, so he continued. 'Give me another minute!'

Brady kept riding for a few more seconds then drew up and turned.

'You've got that minute. Then we ride.'

'Kyle's here,' Dalton said.

Brady looked around the clearing. 'Here? How do you know?'

'It'll take too long to explain and, like you said, I've only got a minute.'

Dalton dismounted and moved towards the bushes where earlier Kyle had spent an inordinate amount of time. Brady grunted at him to wait, but when Dalton carried on he dismounted, then hurried on to join him. He remained quiet as they walked out of the clearing and into the scrub beside the river where Dalton stopped.

'That minute is running out fast,' Brady said.

'Be quiet,' Dalton whispered, taking a pace. 'He's close.'

'How can you. . . ?' Brady broke off when a rustling sounded in the scrub ahead followed by the sight of Kyle running towards the river.

Both men did a double take before Brady got his wits about him and moved off after him. Dalton followed, then slammed into Brady's back when he came to a sudden halt.

'What you doing?' Dalton demanded before he noticed the hole they'd nearly fallen into. A mound of earth was to the side and within the hole lay the crates. 'He was planning to bury them like I thought.'

'You get him,' Brady said approvingly. 'I'll stay with the gold.'

Dalton didn't question his orders, pleased that he'd get to confront Kyle first. He broke into a run, then followed Kyle down the side of the river, but he already had a fifty-yard lead.

Dalton leapt fallen logs and splashed through the shallows, but after 200 yards he hadn't gained on his quarry. He noticed, though, that Kyle was staying close to the river and so that gave him an idea.

The river twisted ahead and so he moved away from the water and sought higher ground. He pushed through the trees and clambered up to a point where the land turned downwards and here he could see the river ahead.

Kyle wasn't visible, but he judged that he'd made

good enough time to come out ahead of him. He hurried down the slope, leaning backwards to avoid falling. He didn't try to move quietly, presuming that as Kyle pushed the undergrowth aside he would make enough noise to mask the progress of his pursuer.

He'd got to within fifty paces of the river when he caught his first sight of Kyle running beside the water, darting glances over his shoulder. As he wasn't looking Dalton's way, Dalton speeded up, aiming to reach him unseen.

Then he put his foot down on a slippery patch of earth and his feet shot from under him. He landed on his back and without control of his movements he slid down the slope, crashing through the undergrowth in an ungainly sprawling manner.

He lost sight of Kyle as he hurled his arms from side to side searching for something to grab hold of and stay his progress, but he failed. The river approached quickly and he could do nothing to stop himself sliding onwards until he plunged into the water feet first.

In the shallows he lay on his back feeling more annoyed and wet than stunned. Then he bounced back to his feet, to stand up to his knees in mud with water draining off him.

Ten feet away Kyle had come to a halt and was looking around, presumably wondering where his other pursuers were.

'Stop!' Dalton demanded, the fall having eroded his last shred of acceptance of Kyle's antics. 'You're surrounded.'

'I'll take my chances,' Kyle said, setting off.

'You won't get far with a bullet in the back.'

Kyle stopped. 'You wouldn't kill me.'

'Don't risk finding out,' Dalton snarled, then waded out of the water. He was unarmed, and Kyle had probably been right, but he figured that in his bedraggled state he might look as if he meant it.

Kyle spread his hands. 'Why are you so angry?'

'Because you left us to face the trouble when you stole the gold.' Dalton paced up to him and slapped a hand on his shoulder. 'But now you'll face that trouble alone while Loren and me head back to Two Forks.'

Kyle gulped, lowering his head in a shamefaced fashion.

'I shouldn't have given in to temptation.'

'You shouldn't.' Dalton gripped his shoulder more tightly, then shepherded him towards Brady and his men. 'But you don't have to explain yourself to me. You do have to explain yourself to the men whose gold you stole.'

'I'll take my punishment for that, but I'm more worried about your and Loren's opinion of me. What will you tell people back at Two Forks?'

Dalton halted. He took several moments to reply, letting his diminishing anger give way to a calmer attitude.

'I guess there's no reason for us to say anything. You made a mistake, but that doesn't have to ruin your new life in Two Forks.' Dalton lowered his voice. 'But if you ever do anything like this again. . . .'

Dalton gave Kyle a significant look to which he responded with a nod. Dalton turned, aiming to head back to the clearing.

He'd taken two steps when a rustling sounded behind him. A moment later a solid blow slammed into the back of his head. The next he knew he was on his knees staring at the earth.

Pattering footsteps sounded, receding as Kyle ran away. Dalton tried to stand but nausea and blurred vision along with a numbness in his limbs overcame him and he flopped down to lie on his side.

How long he lay there he didn't know. The next moment he was aware of anything came when one of Brady's men, Dagwood Brent, dragged him to his feet. Brady stood before him and slapped his face, the unexpected pain shocking him back to full consciousness.

'You fine?' Brady asked.

'I guess,' Dalton murmured.

Brady nodded then turned to Dagwood.

'Get Kyle,' he said. 'I'll get him back to the clearing.'

Dalton accepted Brady's offer of help and with Brady holding him up they headed along the riverside. Before they reached the hole where Kyle had buried the crates he felt well enough to walk alone. He extricated himself from Brady's grip.

When they arrived in the clearing the other men had dragged the crates from the hole and were securing the contents in sacks to take back to the mine encampment.

'You'll not mind if I don't help?' Dalton asked, rubbing the back of his head ruefully.

'Sure,' Brady said. 'You've done enough. Head back while we finish off here.'

Dalton judged that Brady might also not want him around when Dagwood found Kyle, but after what had happened he didn't balk at the thought of the punishment he might mete out.

He returned to his horse and led it upriver towards the mine. After ten minutes of slow walking he had dried off and he felt well enough to mount up, but he still rode on at a walking pace.

He'd almost reached the tree line when Brady and his men joined him. He noted that they didn't have Kyle with them, but he didn't enquire as to whether that meant they'd dealt with him. Without comment he trailed behind them, matching their quicker pace.

When they rode into the encampment Cornelius Gash was waiting for them, standing in the same position as he'd been when they'd left several hours earlier. Even the return of the gold failed to lighten his stern demeanour.

'Where's the thief?' he demanded.

'We almost got him,' Brady said, 'but he escaped. We'll resume the search after we've dropped off the two crates we found.'

Cornelius narrowed his eyes. 'There were three crates.'

Brady shrugged. 'When we find Kyle we'll shake the rest of it out of him.'

'See that you do if you want to carry on working for me.'

'Understood.' Brady gestured for his men to unload the gold.

Dalton watched the exchange with interest. He had been sure he'd seen three crates when he'd nearly fallen into the hole Kyle had dug, but it had been only a quick sighting and, either way, he figured it wasn't his concern.

'And what about him?' Cornelius asked, gesturing at Dalton.

'He didn't lie,' Brady said with approval in his tone. 'He helped us find Kyle, but he doesn't know where he went after he escaped. His usefulness has ended.'

Cornelius nodded then beckoned for Dalton to follow him to the cave in which he was holding Loren. As he made his way up the slope Dalton ran Brady's last comment through his mind, wondering whether it had a sinister intent, but as he still felt groggy he didn't question it any further.

Cornelius stopped before the barred entrance to the cave. While the guard slipped a key in the lock he turned to Dalton.

'You did well,' he said. 'I misjudged you.'

'Can't blame you,' Dalton said. 'You did lose a lot of gold.'

'Still have,' Cornelius said, watching the guard swing open the gate.

Dalton heard two men approach from behind but he ignored them as Loren emerged into the light, blinking with a hand held up to block the low sun. Then he saw Dalton and started to say something, his hand straightening in a warding-off gesture, but he was already too late. The men standing behind Dalton barged him forward, sending him to his knees beyond the opening gate.

The guard swung the gate back, smashing it into the back of Dalton's legs and nudging him along.

Dalton jumped to his feet and threw himself at the bars but the gate had already clanged shut. Two men pressed their boots against the bottom bar and their shoulders against a higher bar to hold the gate still while the guard turned the lock.

'Why?' Dalton shouted, shaking the bars but finding them firm. 'I did everything you asked of me.'

'You've done everything I've asked so far. I might want more from you later.'

With this cryptic comment Cornelius turned away, ignoring Dalton's shouts. Dalton only quietened when Loren placed a hand on his shoulder and bade him follow him into the deeper recesses of the cave.

'I'm sorry,' Loren said as they walked. 'If I'd have heard you coming I'd have told you to escape while you still could.'

'I'd have still come back, but how did you know he'd double-cross me? He can't want anything from us.'

'Except your silence,' a voice said from deeper in the cave.

Dalton turned to see a man emerge from the

darkness. He was stooped and white-haired, and he walked with some difficulty.

'You look as if you've been in here for some time,' Dalton said, considering his frail and emaciated form.

'Only three months, but it gets mighty cold in here at night and with the little they've fed me, it might as well have been three years. For some who've been thrown in here, it's been a lifetime.'

Dalton gulped. 'You mean men get thrown in here to rot?'

'Sure. The town of Durando is a lawless hell-hole but the Durando Mining Company is the worst circle of that particular hell.'

'Is there no way to reason with Cornelius?'

'No.'

'Then his boss?' Dalton waited for an answer, but Loren only uttered a snort while the old man smiled, so he continued: 'This Perry Haynes, the owner of the mine. I've heard he's a reasonable man. Surely he can't accept men being locked up in a cave for no good reason.'

'No. He can't accept that, but that still doesn't mean you'll get out of here.' The man moved closer and lowered his voice to a sympathetic tone. 'Because, you see, I am Perry Haynes, the owner of this here mine.'

CHAPTER 4

'You own all this?' Dalton murmured, aghast.

'I do,' Perry Haynes said. He shuffled over to the side of the cave and sat. 'For now.'

'Who's running it while you're in here?'

'As far as I can tell it's Cornelius with Brady's help, but whether Cornelius is using Brady or Brady is using Cornelius, I can't tell.'

Dalton nodded, then joined Perry who was sitting with his back leaning against the cave wall.

'I know what you mean. Brady claimed we'd found only two of the three missing crates of gold, but I'm sure he's holding out on Cornelius.'

'Then that doesn't give me much hope for your friend's survival, and yours if you let on that you've realized that.'

'I don't care what happens to Kyle no more,' Dalton snapped before he lowered his voice to a more reasonable tone, 'but what happened to you?'

Perry didn't reply immediately as he looked through the cave entrance at the small amount of terrain that was visible to them.

'Ryan Flynn and I founded Durando. He had the money and I had the experience. We shared fairly and paid everyone well, but the mine became too big for me to manage so I hired Cornelius as the overseer. A month later Ryan's head got crushed by a fallen rock in a tunnel. I thought it an accident, but when I called in Owen Muldoon from Durando, he found anomalies. I confronted Cornelius, so he threw me in here and made life hell for the miners, slashing wages, and punishing anyone who complains.'

'Why didn't he kill you?'

'He needed me to sign papers until he could draw up a new contract for the ownership of the mine. When he's done that, he'll dispose of me.'

'How long?'

'Not sure; weeks, perhaps days.'

Dalton paused before asking his unsubtle question, although Loren's sombre expression suggested he wouldn't want to hear the answer.

'And us?' he said, lowering his voice.

'You're alive, so there's hope, and I'd guess that after Brady's lie about the missing gold Cornelius will keep you alive in case you can help him find it. Once he accepts you can't. . . .' Perry sighed. 'Well, there are plenty of dark caves around where nobody will ever find your bodies.'

'Which means,' Loren said, joining them, 'we have to escape.'

Dalton nodded. He looked around the cave.

'Is there any way out?' he asked.

Perry considered him and gave a smile. 'Now that I have you two to help me there is one way out, if you have the courage to try it.'

'Hey,' Dalton shouted through the bars, 'how long do we have to put up with this?'

At first the guard outside the cave ignored him. Then, with the weary air of a man who didn't enjoy his work, he paced over to confront him.

'Be quiet,' he muttered, 'or I'll fetch Cornelius.'

Dalton shrugged and lowered his voice to a more conciliatory tone.

'Just get rid of the body. We don't want to put up with it no more.'

The casual mention of a body made the guard narrow his eyes.

'Body? Who?'

'The old guy. He went an odd colour and collapsed.' Dalton pointed into the dark cave. 'I think he's dead, but I ain't no sawbones.'

The guard considered him, then turned on his heel and called out to men who were out of Dalton's sight.

'Wilson, come here,' he shouted, 'and Luke, fetch Cornelius.'

At the run another man, Wilson, joined the guard.

'He needs help,' Dalton said, 'not Cornelius, but it's up to you.'

Dalton headed to the nearest wall, then leaned against it and waited to see whether they'd take the bait.

The two men muttered to each other, suggesting they wouldn't accept the ruse and open the gate until Cornelius arrived. Dalton was considering how he could dissuade them from waiting when Loren wandered into the light. He noted the men outside weren't making a move to enter. He shrugged.

'Those blotches don't look good,' he said, speaking loudly so the guards could hear. 'I'm staying here in case whatever he's got is catching. I've heard of fevers wiping out whole towns.'

Dalton bunched his jaw, reckoning Loren had pushed their ruse too far, but he obliged with a shiver and cringed away from him.

'I hadn't seen no blotches. Maybe he got 'em off you.'

'Or you,' Loren said, backing away from Dalton.

'That's enough!' the guard outside said, pointing. 'Stand over there while I check him out.'

'Do all the checking you like,' Dalton said. He exchanged a glance with Loren as they moved over to the side of the cave. 'Just get him out.'

The original guard signified that Wilson should watch them while he put a key to the lock and pulled open the gate. After nervously fumbling the key several times he edged inside, walking sideways while watching Dalton and Loren. Then he moved towards the darkened interior.

'Where is he?' he asked, peering ahead.

'Over there,' Dalton said, pointing.

The guard stared into the darkness. When his eyes became accustomed to the lower light level he drew his gun, then slowly paced towards the crumpled figure lying at the back of the cave.

Dalton waited until he was standing over Perry's body. Then he turned to Wilson, standing on the other side of the bars.

'How long will Cornelius be?' he asked.

'What do you want to know that for?' Wilson grunted.

Dalton moved up to the bars. He gripped a bar casually while he glanced over his shoulder into the cave.

'Just want to know when we can start breathing clean air again.'

'If this ain't what you claim, you'll learn what suffering means.'

'We're decent men. We wouldn't kill an old man just to get out.'

This comment appeared to mollify Wilson. He moved closer to the bars while looking at what the other guard was doing, but he stopped two paces back from them.

Dalton also watched the other guard while Loren turned his back on them and stepped backwards until he joined him at the bars. While whistling under his breath Loren reached back to put a hand on the bars as he watched the guard roll Perry on to his side.

'Is he dead?' Wilson asked, edging forward a half-pace in interest.

'Can't tell,' the guard said. 'But he ain't moving.'

He kicked Perry's legs, but that failed to get a

response so he kicked him harder. Then he shrugged and stood to the side to ensure that Perry stayed in the light as he bent towards him. Outside Wilson edged forward again, this time getting to within a pace of the bars.

Perry didn't know that Wilson was now in the right position, but to succeed their plan needed luck along with quick timing. Accordingly when the guard placed a hand on his shoulder to shake him, he shrugged off the hand then swung up a bunched fist and punched the guard in the face.

At that moment Dalton and Loren swung round and hurled their weight against the gate, pushing it outwards and against Wilson. The gate hit him solidly in the chest and knocked him backwards for a pace before he tumbled over. As he hit the ground Dalton ran for the opened side of the gate while Loren hurried back into the cave towards Perry and the guard.

Dalton swung round the side of the gate and dashed towards the sprawling man, who with a shake of the head got his wits about him and, still on his back, drew his gun. But Dalton was on him. He kicked the gun from his hand then dropped down to kneel on his chest.

Wilson tried to buck him away but Dalton delivered a pile-driving punch to his nose. A sickening crack sounded before Wilson's head crashed down into the solid rock. He went limp. Dalton didn't wait to check that he'd knocked him cold, instead he ran for the gun he'd kicked away.

After three long paces he slapped a hand on the weapon then turned towards the cave to see Loren running for the opened cave entrance, a gun in hand. Perry was shuffling along behind.

They met on the other side of the gate.

'You all right?' Dalton asked Perry.

'Three months cooped up in there was a long time,' Perry said, breathing heavily, 'but I'll be fine.'

Dalton nodded. Then they headed away from the cave. High rocks on either side of the entrance stopped them from seeing in advance what kind of opposition they'd face, but they found out soon enough.

They emerged from the rocks to see the route to the encampment entrance, but coming up the hill to the cave was Cornelius and six men. Cornelius halted, then shouted out orders. As one, his men drew their guns.

Faced with so much firepower the three men hurried out of sight.

'Get them,' Cornelius shouted. 'But keep Perry alive.'

Ten yards in front of the gate Loren and Dalton hunkered down and listened to the sounds of Cornelius's men making their way closer, waiting for someone to risk showing himself. Cornelius spoke up from just out of their view.

'You by the cave, you have five seconds to give yourself up or die,' he ordered. 'One . . . Two. . . .'

Dalton looked at Loren, who nodded then he looked at Perry who winked. So when Cornelius's count reached four he and Loren placed their guns on to their palms then threw them overarm towards Cornelius.

'We've given up,' Dalton said with an emphatically resigned sigh as the guns clattered to the ground.

'Be reaching for the sky when I see you and I'll believe you.'

The three men stood and raised their hands. Presently two men edged into view then told Cornelius to join them.

'That was mighty stupid, Perry,' Cornelius said, pacing up to him. 'I've warned you what would happen if you didn't comply. Now you get the pit.'

'Dalton and Loren weren't lying when they said I was ill,' Perry said between grating wheezes that he probably wasn't exaggerating. 'You'd better treat me better or I won't be alive to sign anything.'

'You'll survive because you have something to live for,' Cornelius said, grinning. 'Your daughter's safe, but only while I get what I want.'

Cornelius glared at Perry, then grunted orders. The six men moved in and grabbed each man's arms. Then they roughly marched them away from the cave and up the hill.

When they reached the top, they led them at a quick march over a patch of barren rock to a hollow, at the bottom of which lay a large flat rock. At Cornelius's orders two men released Perry, to leave him standing exhausted and stooped. They tipped the rock up on to its side revealing a gaping four-foot wide hole. Then the men holding Dalton pushed

47

him towards the hole. As he approached Dalton stared down into the void, seeing nothing but darkness below.

'It's fifteen feet down,' Perry shouted to him. 'Brace yourself then move aside quickly to avoid the next one in landing on you.'

'That's good advice,' Cornelius said, 'if you want to come out of there alive. Most don't.'

Dalton gulped as he peered down into the darkness that was to become their new prison.

'You can't keep us down there,' he said.

'You brought this on yourself,' Cornelius murmured without pity. 'You get three days, no light, no food, no water. If you're still alive when we remove the rock, you'll get to enjoy the cave.'

With that promise Cornelius nodded to the men holding Dalton. They shoved him forward, but when they released him Dalton dug in his heels.

He managed to stop himself on the edge and avoided being thrown down into the pit. Then he looked down, the limited light filtering through the hole letting him see the base, fifteen feet below. Then he jumped.

He landed lightly, bounced up, then moved aside to avoid the next man down landing on him. While he waited a quick consideration of his surroundings revealed that the main chamber that was to be their prison for the next three days was around twenty feet wide although there were numerous recesses and crannies.

In short order Loren jumped down followed by

Perry, who landed heavily, but quickly muttered that he was fine. Then they all looked up to see Cornelius looking down at them. With a sneer on his face, he jerked back and issued a quick order.

A few moments later the rock teetered then crashed down over the hole. The fit was tight, the hollow thud like the lid being slammed down on a coffin as, in an instant, they were plunged into absolute darkness.

They heard footfalls above as Cornelius and the others departed. Then they were alone, in the dark.

For five minutes silence reigned. Then, with a clap of his hands, Perry spoke up.

'And so,' he said, 'that completes the easy part of our escape. Are you two ready now for the difficult part?'

CHAPTER 5

The darkness was so complete that Dalton couldn't see his hand when he placed it before his face. So he didn't dare move in any direction for fear of bumping into the wall. Thankfully Perry knew where he was going.

'Stay close,' Perry urged, 'and move slowly.'

Dalton placed a hand on Perry's shoulder and told Loren to keep a hand on his own shoulder. Then they moved off.

Perry took several shuffled paces with his arms outstretched until he reached a wall. He moved to the side, scraping his hand across the rock, then resumed shuffling forward.

Dalton gritted his teeth, assuming they'd walk into the rockface, but Perry moved until Dalton's boots and then his shoulders scraped rock.

'How far?' Dalton asked, his voice echoing back at him from close to.

'A lot further and lower your head,' Perry said, making Dalton jerk downwards so swiftly it made him chuckle. 'If you're nervous, raise an arm to feel the rock.'

Dalton did so, but he moved too quickly and banged his fist against the cave roof. When the numbness had subsided it felt comforting to know where his boundaries were.

He felt the roof and judged they were in a thin recess. Although it widened after a few paces, in the darkness Dalton sensed that the walls were inches from his face and any sideways movement would knock him against rock. But they walked on steadily, taking one slow pace at a time.

'Why doesn't Cornelius know about this way out?' Dalton asked, more to alleviate his own concern as he'd asked this question earlier.

'He never gets his hands dirty. He explored a few holes, saw they went nowhere and assumed there was no way out, but I've been over every inch of this hill above and below ground. There are natural tunnels here that he'd never find even if he came here with a torch.'

'Who else knows the layout down here as well as you do?'

'Hopefully,' Perry said with laughter in his voice, 'the other people he put in here who didn't come out.'

Dalton gave a supportive grunt, then in silence they paced on for several minutes until Loren spoke up.

'One thing you didn't tell us about, Perry,' he said. 'Your daughter.'

51

Perry drew in a long breath and came to a sudden halt, making Dalton walk into him.

'Mattie was a mistake,' he said. 'Well, not in having her, but in bringing her here. I thought I could keep her safe if she was with me, but when Cornelius took over the mine he seized her. I haven't seen her since.'

'I hope he's holding her somewhere better than down here.'

'It depends on how you look at it. Houston Floyd in Durando has her now. The threat is that if I don't sign the documents he gives me. . . .'

'Houston kills her?' Loren asked when Perry didn't continue.

'There are worse fates for a young woman in a town like Durando.'

Dalton gripped Perry's shoulder then nudged him forward.

'When we get out of here we'll make sure she doesn't suffer no more.'

Perry got the hint and continued walking.

They stayed silent, taking one steady pace at a time, usually forwards but also taking sudden sideways and downwards movements. Only occasionally did they move upwards.

As their progress was slow and there was little else to occupy his mind, Dalton made a mental note of their changes in direction. He doubted his memory would be good enough to find this escape route if he needed to use it again, but it took his mind off the disturbing process of spending so much time underground in darkness.

They walked through an open space where every footstep echoed far away. Then Dalton heard water rushing by to his right, after which they squeezed through a narrow gap that they wouldn't have managed if any of them had been overweight.

Throughout Perry maintained an unerring onward movement that gave Dalton confidence that he knew where he was going.

The darkness had become so constant that he was surprised when he saw something move ahead. At first he thought it to be a trick of his sensory deprivation, but then the movement came again and he realized that it was Perry's outline.

'Can you see that?' he said.

'I can,' Loren murmured behind him. 'We must be near the surface.'

'We are,' Perry said, 'so be quiet. We don't know who's out there.'

With more confidence they speeded up and the light level grew until Dalton could see the sides of the tunnel and the place that they would ultimately reach. And it appeared to be a dead end.

He kept those thoughts to himself, trusting in Perry's uncanny ability to find a route to safety, but when Perry called a halt he saw that his concern was justified. The way ahead stopped at a rock face with no detours to the left or right. He was about to ask what they did next when the obvious thought came.

He looked up and above him was a crooked chimney, although he couldn't see the top.

'I said this wouldn't be easy,' Perry said, noting

53

Dalton's concern.

Perry shooed them away then placed a hand on the wall. He located a handhold, drew himself off the ground and climbed.

Dalton and Loren watched his route while casting glances at each other that acknowledged how impressed they were. Previously Perry had appeared to be a frail old man but, with freedom getting close, the fortitude that had got him through three months of imprisonment was showing itself.

Perry moved carefully until he edged out of sight beyond a sharp turn in the chimney. A thud sounded and a moment later he peered down at them. With a finger to his lips he pointed at the wall, signifying that they should join him.

Dalton followed first. Once he'd found the first handhold he manoeuvred himself up the slope quickly until he found Perry lying on a wide ledge that blocked most of the chimney. He swung on to the ledge and lay on his side, catching his breath while Perry gestured at Loren to join them.

Here it was lighter than below and when he looked up he saw the twilit red sky and clouds drifting by.

The sight was so pleasing that for a moment it distracted him from noticing that although freedom was only twenty feet away the walls that they would have to climb up were smooth. Worse, the hole closed up, meaning that the climber would have to lean backwards to reach the surface. Worst of all, moisture was running down the sides.

'Have you ever climbed it?' Dalton asked Perry.

'Not without a rope.' Perry pointed. 'But there's a discarded winch on that side. When you reach the surface you can grab hold of it and pull yourself out.'

Dalton stood. He saw the top of the winch, but he couldn't see how to reach it and when Loren joined him, he too stood in exasperated silence.

'This is impossible,' he murmured at last. 'Just a few feet but no way to cover them.'

'Nothing is impossible until it's been tried,' Dalton said.

'That's right,' Loren said, brightening. 'Maybe it won't be as hard as it looks.'

Dalton smiled at the positive thinking but by the time they had all tried and failed twice he had decided Loren was right. It wasn't as hard as it looked. It was harder.

Each time they managed to raise themselves only once before the lack of handholds and the slippery rock sent them tumbling down on to the ledge. The last time Loren scraped his hand, but when he dabbed it with a scrunched-up length of his vest to make the bleeding stop, Dalton had an idea.

'We need rope,' he said, 'and as we haven't got one, we need to make one.'

Loren started to ask Dalton what he meant, but stopped when Dalton slipped off his jacket.

Ten minutes later the three men were shivering in their underclothes, but they had twenty feet of makeshift rope made from tied-together jackets and trousers.

Dalton faced the winch, then hurled the rope. The first effort went only a few feet in the air. The second hit the wall. The third hurtled upwards, but the rope slipped from his hand. Everyone watched it rise then come coiling down on to the ledge.

With an embarrassed cough, Dalton took more care over his next attempt. His failures had let him work out how to throw the rope properly. The end went through the hole, then rested on the winch. They watched with bated breath until the weight of the rope below dragged it down and it coiled down to land on their heads.

But his near-success had heartened them. With whispered encouragement ringing in his ears Dalton tried again, and again, and again until finally one throw sent the rope through the hole, for it flop down out of sight.

This time it stayed put.

Dalton tentatively tugged on the end, but the rope didn't move.

'It's snagged,' he said. 'Who's trying it?'

'The lightest,' Perry said, stepping forward.

'The strongest,' Loren said, shaking his head.

Loren and Perry faced each other, aiming to argue their case, but Dalton pointed at Loren, ending the discussion.

To reduce the amount of time Loren would be suspended Dalton knelt. Then Loren sat on his shoulders and when Dalton had stood and braced himself against the wall, he clambered up to stand on his shoulders. This manoeuvre got his raised hands over half the way to the chimney top. Then he had no option but to risk that the rope had snagged on something that would hold his weight.

The sides were too smooth and slippery to use them for leverage, so Loren grabbed the rope in both hands and tugged himself up. His feet left Dalton's shoulders and he swung out to dangle in the centre of the hole.

Dalton and Perry held their arms out ready to break Loren's fall, but he stayed put. Then he tugged himself up, going hand over hand.

Five firm pulls dragged him up to within a few feet of the edge, but then the inevitable happened. A ripping sound echoed. Loren slipped down then jerked to a halt a few feet lower. But the ripping continued.

'Get up now!' Dalton urged. 'We won't get another chance.'

Loren threw himself up the rope, lunging with firm pulls, getting closer to the top with every movement. Then the rope gave way. The clothes tumbled down on the men below, but Loren launched himself away from the makeshift rope and hurled out a hand to grab the edge.

He dangled one-handed, his legs swinging free. Then he threw up his left hand and got a secure hold of the winch.

He held himself there then drew his body up until his chin was above the hole. He planted an elbow on the ground before swinging himself up to get a leg on the surface.

Then he rolled from sight. A few moments passed before more items of clothing came tumbling down on them. Then Loren's beaming face emerged.

'Nobody's around,' he reported, 'but it ain't all good news. Someone's jacket has lost an arm and someone's pants will be real draughty.'

Dalton and Perry laughed. Then Loren set about getting them out. Using Perry's explanation of the layout of the land he crept off.

'Do he think he'll find anything?' Dalton asked.

'The hole comes out outside the mine,' Perry said, 'but people do throw things away.'

Perry's sceptical sneer suggested this was unlikely to be the case. Sure enough when Loren returned he reported that he hadn't found any rope and he didn't want to risk drawing attention to himself by searching.

Dalton and Perry had already guessed this would be the case and had remade the rope. Since it would now not be now necessary to snag the winch they had made it thicker than before.

Dalton threw an end up to Loren, then, with Loren bracing himself, he dragged himself off the ground. He wasn't as quick as Loren had been but he reached the top without mishap.

Then it was Perry's turn.

The unspoken thought on Dalton's mind was that this part of their escape plan might turn out to be problematic, but he hoped that the old and weak man would summon up a last reserve of strength.

He was wrong.

Perry flexed his arms, then pulled, but he remained on the ledge. After several attempts he shook his head, so Dalton and Loren took the strain while Perry held the rope. They got his feet off the ledge, but then his hands slipped and he tumbled down to sit looking forlornly up at them.

Even more worryingly he was shivering uncontrollably. Now that the sun had set the temperature had dropped sharply. After two more failed attempts Loren leaned towards Dalton.

'He has to get out now or he never will,' he whispered.

'I know,' Dalton said, slapping his arms and rocking from foot to foot as he fought to stay warm.

So they sent down a changed set of instructions, after which Perry wrapped the rope around his chest and under his arms. Loren and Dalton took the strain, then drew him up.

Foot by foot they raised him. They got him to within five feet of ground level, then a knot slipped. The rope stretched and jerked to a halt.

The two men froze, waiting and hoping that the rope would hold, but the strain on the other knots was too great and the rope unravelled.

'Let him down,' Loren urged.

They reversed their previous motion and lowered Perry to the ledge. Then the rope gave way, the release of tension sending both men tumbling backwards as down below a sickening thud sounded.

Both men winced. They looked over the edge to see Perry lying on his back.

'I'm fine,' Perry murmured, raising a hand. 'Nothing's broken.'

'We'll do better next time,' Dalton said.

'There won't be a next time,' Perry said through chattering teeth. He coughed painfully. 'I'm too weak for this.'

After a quick consultation Dalton and Loren decided to resolve their most pressing problem. They dismantled the rope so they could all get dressed, but even when Perry felt warmer he was still pessimistic about his chances of getting out. Several items of their clothing had been too badly torn to make a viable rope and the painful bump he had received had knocked away the last of his resolve.

'We'll find proper rope,' Dalton said.

'Forget about rope,' Perry said, some of his former confidence returning. 'All that matters is my daughter. Get to Durando. Get her away from Houston Floyd. Only then need you worry about getting me out of here.'

'We can't leave you,' Dalton said as Loren grunted his support.

'You can. I'm weak. I'll only slow you down, and besides I've survived for three months in these caves. I can wait for another day.'

'All right,' Dalton said. 'But we know nothing about Durando.'

'Houston Floyd is easy to find. He runs the biggest and rowdiest saloon in town.' Perry paused to consider for a moment. 'And the nearest that town has to the law, and an honourable man, is Owen

Muldoon. When Cornelius killed Ryan, he helped me work out what had happened, so seek him out. If he won't help you, you're on your own.'

Loren and Dalton looked at each other, sighing at the thought of the difficult task ahead. Then, after urging Perry to stay calm and resolute, they turned their backs on the mine to face the darkening western horizon.

Ahead was the one place neither man had wanted to visit: the lawless hell-hole that was Durando.

CHAPTER 6

Dalton looked into the gathering gloom and noted that Perry had described the terrain correctly. The hole from which they'd emerged was on the opposite side of the hill to the mine entrance.

On this side the ridge itself was either vertical or overhanging, providing a natural barrier. After they'd considered it for ten minutes they decided it was unguarded. So they headed away without too much concern about being seen.

After a mile they circled round to head by the pass leading to the mine. By the time the gibbous moon had risen and was scudding behind low cloud they reached a heavily rutted trail. Neither man knew for sure where the trail went, but it was a reasonable assumption that Durando would be at one end.

They used the moon to orient themselves and took the direction that moved them away from the river. They trudged on into the night. Aside from night animals they didn't hear or so see anyone until, after they'd been walking for an hour, a wagon trundled closer from behind.

They slipped off the trail, but when the wagon passed them they saw it was only full of raucous singing men. They judged that these men were miners heading to town for some well-earned rest. So, with greater hope of their being close to their destination, they headed on.

After another half-mile they saw lights ahead and the sounds of revelry drifted to them along with the occasional gunshot. They hoped that these had been fired in good spirits. Gradually Durando opened up to them. It was as unpromising a town as they'd expected.

The only permanent building was the wooden saloon. That was a ramshackle one-storey construction. It had walls that sloped so steeply it appeared as ready to tip over as two propped-up playing cards.

This building was the only well-lit structure, and most of the noise was emanating from it. Littering the main drag were grimy tents from which furtive men and dead-eyed women emerged to gesture at people passing by, each offering a different inducement to enter and spend their money.

Many of the miners who had passed them earlier were dispersing to make their choices, but around ten men were still standing beside the wagon. They had been talking but the sight of two men walking into town drew their attention and they turned to silently watch Dalton and Loren approach.

Both men nodded in their direction before they

headed for the wooden building, assuming that this represented their best chance of finding out about both Houston Floyd and Owen Muldoon.

They stopped outside to gather their torn and tattered clothing about them, hoping that their ragged state would mean they'd not look too out of place amongst the grimy miners. Then they moved to the door, but a strident voice barked out from behind, halting them.

'What you two doing?'

Dalton assumed they were being challenged with a view to persuading them to waste their money in one of the tents, so when he turned words of refusal were on his lips. But he found he was facing two of the miners from the wagon. He noted that the rest of the miners were walking by, aiming to head further into town, but these two remained to glare at them with eagerness lighting their eyes.

'Looking for entertainment,' Dalton said, 'same as you.'

'Two dandied up men walk into a town like Durando,' the second man said with a sneer. 'You ain't looking for the same as us.'

Dalton couldn't help but laugh as he spread out his torn jacket.

'You couldn't exactly call us dandied up.' He smiled in the hope of receiving a smile in return, but this comment only went to annoy the men.

'You making fun of us?' the second man demanded.

'No, I. . . .' Dalton sighed while looking aloft, then

glanced at Loren, who shrugged.

'He's right,' Loren said, keeping his voice low so the men wouldn't hear him. 'We do look out of place. Perhaps a change of clothes might help us fit in.'

Dalton nodded, seeing the sense of what Loren was suggesting, then with Loren at his side he paced up to the men.

'Yeah, I *was* making fun of you,' he said, raising his voice to a belligerent tone, 'except you're too damn pig-headed to understand. Must be all that banging your head on—'

Dalton didn't get to finish his insult when the nearest man roared with anger. He stormed up to him, then swung back his fist ready to deliver a haymaker of a punch to Dalton's face. But Dalton had already prepared himself for that action. He thundered a low punch into the man's guts that had him folding over, bleating in pain.

Dalton danced back a pace as Loren tussled with his opponent. Dalton put him from his mind and waited for the man to straighten. Then he moved in and thudded a short-armed jab to the man's chin that cracked his head back. Then he delivered a two-handed swipe to his cheek that toppled him.

The man landed on his side, tried to get up, but he was still stunned. He slumped back down on to his rump and sat shaking his head. Dalton gave him no time to regain his senses. He kicked out, slamming the side of his boot against the man's temple and pole-axing him.

He swirled round to see how Loren was faring. He saw him standing over the limp body of the second man with a fist bunched. When he was sure the man wouldn't move Loren turned his back on him.

'Today has been a mighty tough one,' he said, batting his hands together and smiling, 'but that sure felt good.'

Dalton gave a supportive laugh. Then they grabbed each man's legs and dragged them around the side of the saloon.

Five minutes later they had shed their own ragged clothing and had donned a new, albeit rank-smelling and dirty set of clothes. A quick rub of dirt on their hands and faces let them appear to be scruffy as most of the denizens of Durando were. With more confidence they headed into the saloon.

The inside was as raucous as they'd expected. By the door two men were arguing over a saloon girl and they had to crane their necks to see round them into the main room. There, the bar took up one wall and before it a crowd of miners pushed and shoved as they jockeyed for position.

No tables or chairs were in the main area, the only sitting space being a raised dais at the back on which a dozen men sat around two large tables. From the door it was clear that the miners left a space of several yards around the dais and that they had purposely turned their backs on the men sitting there.

One man sat alone to the left of the dais, eyeing the chaos from under a lowered hat. He was large, his bloated belly bulging so much it strained his buttons apart. He was also the most smartly dressed of the people here. To avoid being seen staring at him Dalton leaned towards Loren.

'I'd judge that he's the saloon owner Houston Floyd,' he said.

'Or he's someone in authority who'll know how we'll find him,' Loren replied, 'although I reckon it'll be best to find Owen Muldoon first.'

Dalton nodded. He looked around for someone whom he could ask without drawing suspicion on himself, but before he saw anyone suitable the two arguing men nudged into him.

'Hey,' one man said, pushing him away, 'you ain't having her first either.'

'I don't want her,' Dalton said, raising his hands. 'I only came here to see Owen Muldoon. You know where he is?'

The man sneered. 'He won't be interested in your problems. Sort them out for yourself.'

Dalton shrugged, then advanced a long pace on him.

'If you don't know where he is, then maybe I do have the time to take the girl first.'

The man considered the firm set of Dalton's shoulders, then he noticed that Loren was at his side and that he had six inches on him. He gulped and a nervous glance over his shoulder confirmed the other man had taken advantage of the distraction to monopolize the saloon girl. So with a wave of a hand he dismissed the matter, then pointed to the right side of the dais.

'Owen is the tall man sitting at the opposite end to Houston Floyd,' he said.

Dalton grunted his thanks. With this information gathered they left the two men to settle their argument over the girl and made their way towards the dais. From the positioning of the men sitting around Owen's table, with Owen facing the saloon and the others flanking him, Dalton presumed they worked for him.

'We just going straight up to him?' Loren asked.

'Got no choice,' Dalton said. 'He's already noticed us.'

Loren winced. He looked over to see that Owen was watching their progress with interest. Dalton met his gaze as he moved to step up on to the dais but, in a blur of motion, two of the seated men swung off their chairs.

'That's near enough,' one man said, grabbing his right arm, halting him while the second man frisked him for a weapon. A third man did the same to Loren.

'We want to talk to you about a problem,' Dalton said when they'd released him.

'Any problem that happens in my town,' Owen said, 'interests me.'

'This happened before we got here.'

'Then it's no concern of mine.' Owen pointed into the main saloon area. 'Go.'

'We ain't going nowhere.' Dalton stamped his feet to the floor and folded his arms in a show of his staying put. Loren matched his action.

Owen deliberately looked away from them but when they continued to wait he gave a grunted snarl, kicked out two spare chairs and beckoned for them to sit.

The men around the table changed position to let Dalton and Loren sit opposite Owen, but each man stared at them with a steady menace that said they should state their business quickly.

'So,' Owen said, 'is this to do with the men you assaulted?'

Dalton flinched, taken aback by this question.

'Men?'

Owen snorted. 'Nothing that happens in my town passes me by and especially nothing done by you two. You walk into town in rags, assault the first two men you meet, steal their clothing, then come looking for me. Unless you've got a mighty good story to tell, before those two come round I'll be running you out of town.'

'I'm impressed,' Dalton said. He glanced along the dais at Houston who wasn't showing any interest in this conversation. 'But I understood that if anyone could lay claim to this being their town, it was him.'

Owen smiled. 'Houston still does, but maybe not for long. A whole heap of his men left town earlier this week and haven't returned, so right now he's depending on me and that makes me the one in control.'

'Control? I'd heard you weren't interested in controlling anyone. I'd heard you were the nearest

Durando has to a decent and honourable man.'

'Who said that?'

'Perry Haynes.'

Owen narrowed his eyes then nodded slowly.

'He was right. I deal with everyone in a just way, even if they don't deserve it.' Owen gestured around the saloon, taking in the teeming miners before ending at Houston. 'He and the owners of the other more dubious establishments pay me to keep the peace in Durando, and I do, but before I came here, men died almost daily: shot, stabbed, lynched. . . .'

'And now?'

'Men still die, but everyone knows what'll happen if I see them break my rules, and I miss nothing. But no matter who was to blame everyone knows I hold no grudges and grant no favours, so state your business.'

Dalton ran this statement through his mind and judged that it was fair by the standards he'd expected to find in Durando. He took a deep breath before he replied.

'The Durando Mining Company is no longer run by Perry Haynes. After Ryan Flynn was murdered, Cornelius. . . .' Dalton noted that Owen was frowning while looking around in a bored manner. 'But you already know that!'

'I sure do and as I told you, it ain't got nothing to do with me. I look after Durando. Others can deal with whatever happens elsewhere.'

'But you helped Perry.'

'I did what I was paid to do.' Owen shrugged.

'Nothing more.'

Dalton sneered. 'Then I made a mistake. You're not the man I thought you were.'

Around the table Owen's men muttered with irritation, then edged forwards. Owen raised a hand and bade them to back away.

'You can insult me once, but no man has ever done it twice. Go back to where you came from before you annoy me again.'

Dalton scraped back his chair and stood up. He moved to go, but Loren had stayed sitting.

'I haven't insulted or annoyed you,' he said using a tone that in the circumstances was surprisingly soft. 'So answer me one question before we go.'

'Which is?' Owen asked, still looking at Dalton.

'Mattie Haynes, Perry's daughter, where is she?'

Owen swung his gaze sideways to transfix Loren, his narrowed eyes and grinding jaw conveying that he was thinking and perhaps discerning their true purpose in coming to Durando. He gave a slight smile.

'You've already met her.'

'We've met no women since we came here.'

'But you have.' Owen leaned forward and pointed to the door where the two miners were still bartering over a saloon girl. 'Perry's daughter is the saloon girl by the door, and she's about to start another long and demanding night keeping the miners happy.'

CHAPTER 7

'That can't be her,' Loren murmured as he and Dalton stepped down from the dais.

Dalton sighed, deciding that Loren had meant he had hoped rather than known the saloon girl wasn't Perry Haynes's daughter.

'There's only way to find out,' he said, 'but let me do the talking and don't do anything to attract Houston Floyd's attention.'

Loren nodded and slipped back to let Dalton take the lead. As they crossed the saloon area the business between the miners and the saloon girl concluded with one miner heading to the bar while the other moved to the door with the girl. Dalton hurried to catch up with them, but they slipped outside while he was still struggling to extract himself from the crowd.

This didn't disappoint him as it meant they could resolve matters while not being watched by either Houston or Owen. By the time he pushed through the door, the twosome was heading down the road towards a group of tents on the edge of town.

Dalton glanced to the side of the saloon to confirm that the men they'd accosted earlier were still where they'd left them, then hurried off. So many people were making their way about town that neither of the pair reacted to his approaching footfalls. When he reached them he slapped a hand on the departing miner, halting him, then swung him round.

'What you want this time?' the miner muttered.

Dalton settled his stance as he waited for Loren to join him.

'Her,' he grunted, matching the miner's surly demeanour and tone.

'Sheckley's paid for me,' the saloon girl said. 'Get back inside.'

Her tired and defeated voice made Dalton wince and he hoped again that he'd been wrong about who she was, but her comment bolstered her client's confidence.

'Yeah,' Sheckley said. 'Like she said, wait your turn.'

Sheckley turned away, but it was to find that Loren had side-stepped around him to block his way.

'We ain't doing that,' Loren said, keeping his tone pleasant to give the miner a chance to back down. 'Now go back to the saloon and find another one while you can still walk there.'

Sheckley rubbed his jaw, weighing up his chances; but as Dalton and Loren squared their stances then moved in towards him, he chose discretion and backed away for a pace while raising his hands.

'You'd better hope she's worth it,' he muttered, 'because there's plenty of dark tunnels back at the mine.'

'We sure know that,' Dalton said ruefully.

He waited until he was sure that Sheckley was returning to the saloon before turning to the saloon girl, but he saw none of the relief in her demeanour that he'd hoped to see. Instead, she was staring at them, fear making her eyes glow brightly in the light filtering from the saloon.

'Don't hurt me,' she murmured with a quaver in her voice that she tried hard to suppress, 'or Houston Floyd won't like it.'

Dalton softened his voice as much as he could.

'We won't harm you, Mattie.'

Her eyes narrowed slightly, suggesting he had correctly named her, but the fear remained.

'Being nice won't get you nothing extra either. Pay up or I'm going back to the saloon.'

Dalton looked around, noting the numerous people out on the road. Presumably many of them worked for Owen Muldoon, bearing in mind the ease with which he'd kept track of their earlier activities.

Absently he patted his pockets. He smiled when he discovered that the miner he'd accosted had brought funds for his night of entertainment. He held out a handful of coins and let her take her fee. Then, with a glance at Loren to confirm he was happy with following through with the charade, he let her lead him down the road, as if nothing was untoward.

She stopped and listened outside three sets of tent

74

flaps before leading him into the fourth tent. Dalton stayed back to bid Loren to stay outside and make sure nobody came close, then followed her in.

A quick perusal of the inside showed that this was a communal tent containing no personal effects. A rough tangle of blankets lay on the ground, a single chair faced him, and a crude table on which stood a water jug and bowl was to his side.

'Get clean,' she said with contempt while she turned her back on him to light a candle, 'while I get ready for you.'

Dalton sighed. 'I'm not here for that. I want to talk.'

'I don't. Get it over with, then get out of here.'

Dalton reached out to place a comforting hand on her shoulder. Then he decided that it would only make her more fearful and withdrew his hand.

'I can't believe Houston's done this to you. He was supposed to be keeping you safe.'

'Do you know me?' she murmured, her voice breaking with the first sign of hope as she turned on her heel to face him.

'Not you, your father.'

She shrieked before putting her hand to her mouth, her eyes opening wide and watering in the candlelight.

'Please tell me that Houston didn't send you to torture me more with stories of hope. I couldn't cope with that.'

'No stories. I've come from the mine to take you away.'

75

'But you can't. Cornelius is holding my father as a virtual prisoner. Houston says that if I try to leave Durando, Cornelius will kill him. I have to do everything he asks of me.'

Dalton looked aloft, sighing as he considered and then rejected several versions of the truth that might soften her misery before deciding she'd been lied to enough.

'Houston lied. Your father isn't a *virtual* prisoner. He *is* a prisoner! He was told that if he co-operated you'd be kept safe and not turned into a . . . a. . . .'

She lowered her head and uttered a sob, stumbling slightly. Dalton moved to catch her, but she raised a hand and shook her head.

'I'll be fine,' she croaked in a broken voice that suggested she'd be anything but. 'I'm pleased you told me the truth, but that still doesn't change the fact that I can't leave Durando or Cornelius will kill him.'

'Don't worry. We have a plan to make this all work out right.' Dalton smiled and maintained that expression when she looked up, hoping she would return a smile of her own, while offering a silent prayer that she didn't ask what that plan was.

In truth they hadn't thought through their actions beyond the need to get her out of town and getting rope to help Perry escape from the pit. But now that they'd achieved their first objective in finding Mattie he had to admit that on foot without weapons or allies, achieving their further aims wouldn't be simple.

76

Luckily she didn't ask for details and instead offered a comment that was more sensible than he could have hoped for in the circumstances.

'I've put up with a lot over the last few months,' she said, gaining some assurance in her tone. 'All that's kept me alive is the hope that everything would turn out well in the end. Now that I know there are more good men here like my father, I'll bide awhile. Don't worry about me. Just tell me when you're ready to act and I'll leave with you.'

Dalton nodded, worried that she would have to endure her predicament for a while longer, but pleased that she'd given him time to work out a way to resolve matters carefully. He rummaged in his pockets and found that the miner he'd assaulted had collected over twenty dollars.

'Loren and I will pay for as much of your time as we can, perhaps all of it, and we'll get you away from here as soon as possible.'

'I know you will,' Mattie said, placing a hand on his arm.

Dalton gestured to the chair, inviting her to sit while he thought through his problems, but before he could begin, Loren jerked his head through the tent flap.

'You need to see this,' he urged. 'It's Kyle Mallory. He's come to town too and he's in big trouble.'

This news made Dalton snort with derision, but he bade Mattie stay where she was, then joined Loren outside. The animated activity that had been taking place on the main drag had lessened with everyone

77

stopping to watch their treacherous erstwhile companion run down the centre of the road.

He was veering from side to side looking for a suitable place to hide while five riders galloped after him. Dalton and Loren both recognized his pursuers at the same time. Quickly they slipped backwards into the tent to watch while keeping themselves hidden.

'Brady Cox!' Dalton said as he watched the riders bear down on the scurrying Kyle. 'I'm surprised he bothered to chase him like he told Cornelius he would.'

'Kyle doesn't have the gold Brady kept for himself. Brady has to silence him.'

Dalton winced. 'Then this sure is going to be ugly, but nothing less than he deserves.'

Loren shook his head. 'No man deserves to be hunted down like this.'

'You're more forgiving than I am,' Dalton murmured. He felt the bump on his head, then kept silent as he watched the developing situation.

When Kyle reached the saloon the riders spread out. Two galloped on ahead to block Kyle's route out of town; not that there was anywhere to run to there. Three riders grouped on the other side to block him while Brady came towards him in the middle, aiming to be the one who captured him. He grinned as the chase reached its final stage. He dismounted then walked towards Kyle.

Frantically Kyle searched for an escape route, running towards the horses to the left then to the right before being shepherded back. He took one look at the advancing Brady, then turned on his heel and ran to the saloon, the only available direction that would let him remain free, albeit for only seconds. But then he skidded to a halt as two men paced out through the door: Owen Muldoon and Houston Floyd.

Dalton presumed he'd never met either man before but their presence made the frightened Kyle place his arms up before his face as if to ward off a blow before he turned on his heel. For the first time he looked towards the tent where Dalton and Loren were hiding. Even from a hundred yards away Dalton could see the fear in his eyes as he experienced what would probably be his last moments of freedom.

From the purposeful set of Brady's shoulder, it was probably set to be his last moments of life too.

The desperation of the situation lent Kyle a manic burst of energy. He unexpectedly ran at Brady, catching him off guard. He barged him aside then ran down the road, heading for the tents.

'He ain't got a hope,' Loren murmured, shaking his head sadly.

'Just delaying the inevitable,' Dalton agreed, watching Kyle run towards them.

Being pushed over soured Brady's delighted mood. With brisk gestures he ordered the two nearest riders to run Kyle down. Both men set off after the running Kyle. One man hurried on ahead to pass him, then stopped at the tent beside the one in which Dalton and Loren were hiding. There he swirled his horse round to block Kyle's planned route.

The second rider bore down on his quarry and when Kyle skidded to a halt and turned, aiming to find a new escape route, he launched himself from the saddle. He caught Kyle around the neck, his momentum throwing them both into the tent, which collapsed around them.

Their movement took them out of Dalton's view. So he and Loren searched the sides of the tent until they found holes to look through and watch how Kyle fared next. It was to see that his dash for freedom had reached its inevitable end.

The tent now lay flat except for the mounds created by the sparse furniture. Kyle lay propped up against one of those mounds with his assailant kneeling on his legs while gripping his neck with a firm hand. His other hand was held back and bunched, the blood flowing down Kyle's face showing that he'd been punched on the nose. The threat was clear that he'd be hit again if he resisted.

Brady slowed as he approached the tent, now smiling again.

'You did well,' he said, although his cold and pitiless voice didn't sound admiring. 'I've hunted men for years and none of them ever got away. You shouldn't have bothered trying.'

'There was no need to hound me,' Kyle said, his voice high-pitched and scared. 'I left the gold.'

Brady snorted a laugh then gave a brief gesture that made his other men dismount and stand around their quarry.

'That's an interesting story,' he said. 'And one you'll regret repeating.'

Brady gestured at the man holding Kyle, who released his grip and moved backwards to get out of the way. Then Brady drew his gun.

'I was right,' Loren murmured inside the tent. 'Brady tracked him down to silence him. We have to do something.'

Loren moved towards the tent flap, but Dalton swung round and grabbed his arm.

'We're unarmed. There's nothing we can do but get ourselves killed. Besides, Kyle brought this on himself when he turned on us, twice.'

'That still don't mean I'm prepared to stand by and watch a man get killed in cold blood.'

'But what about Perry and Mattie?'

Loren shot a look at Mattie, his sudden movement suggesting he'd forgotten about their main aim, but to Dalton's surprise Mattie shook her head.

'Forget me,' she said. 'Pa wouldn't want you to let a decent man die just to save himself, or me.'

'Decent!' Dalton snorted, but with Mattie and Loren both looking at him, a pang of conscience hit him and he opened his hand, releasing Loren's arm. 'All right, but what—?'

'That's enough!' the strident voice of Owen Muldoon shouted outside.

Dalton hurried back to the hole to look out. He saw that Owen was advancing across the road towards the fallen tent. Behind him Houston Floyd had stopped in the middle of the road while several of Owen's men were spreading out, each man positioning himself close to one of Brady's men in case Brady ignored his demand.

'Stay out this,' Brady said, still holding his gun on the cowering Kyle.

'Can't do that, Brady,' Owen said. 'You know my rules.'

'I can't believe you're still taking orders from Houston Floyd.'

Owen stopped walking, then glanced over his shoulder to see that Houston was staying in the middle of the road.

'I'm not,' he said, lowering his voice, 'and I can't believe you're still taking orders from Cornelius Gash.'

Brady rubbed his jaw then lowered his gun.

'I'm not.'

'Then perhaps we have more in common than either of us would like to admit.'

Brady snorted a rueful laugh. 'Cornelius runs the mine and Houston runs Durando, and yet Cornelius relies on me and Houston relies on you.'

For long moments Brady looked at Owen. Although Dalton knew little of the history that had got these men into positions of power, he gathered that a familiar debate was being touched upon, albeit using a guarded choice of words. Clearly Brady was planning to move in on Cornelius soon in the same way that Cornelius had moved in on Perry, and perhaps Owen had the same view about Houston.

'Houston pays me to keep the peace in Durando,' Owen said, 'and I will. You won't kill this man in my territory.'

Brady considered Owen. Slowly a smile spread.

'Then maybe I should take him out of town.'

Owen narrowed his eyes, bunched his fists. Dalton hoped that if Perry had been correct and Owen was a decent man, the conclusion to this debate would be that Owen would take Kyle into custody and safety. But that hope fled when Owen backed away a pace and heaved a resigned sigh.

'Do as you will. Whatever happens out of town is no concern of mine, only what happens in Durando.'

'I understand.' Brady gestured to the man standing before Kyle. The man grabbed Kyle's shoulder and yanked him to his feet. 'You won't get no arguments from me when I'm in Durando.'

Owen nodded, noting his emphasis. 'Then I'm pleased this situation arose so we could get to understand each other's boundaries.'

'For now and for the future,' Brady said, smirking. Then he turned away from Owen and gestured for rope.

Quickly rope was passed over and Kyle's hands were tied. Then Brady and his men turned to lead him out of town towards what would be an inevitable and cruel end.

Kyle shot a beseeching look at Owen, but he wouldn't meet his eye. Then he looked along the road, taking in the bystanders, but none of them appeared interested enough in his plight to intervene.

Dalton couldn't bear to watch this situation play itself out. He backed away from the hole to find that Loren had already moved away. He was looking at him, conveying his thoughts on the matter with his firm-set jaw and his brooding furrowed brow.

Dalton spread his hands and offered a consoling smile.

'If there was anything we could do . . .' he said, but that only made Loren flare his eyes.

'That don't make it any easier,' he grunted.

Mattie stepped between the two men.

'If you want to help him,' she offered, 'I could provide a distraction.'

Dalton shook his head. 'You need to stay out of trouble until we can get you out of here.'

'But she's right,' Loren murmured as, outside, Kyle screeched and the sounds of a brief scuffle came to them. Then they heard him being dragged past their tent, struggling at every pace. 'We have to help him. If we do nothing, we're no better than Owen is.'

That last comment decided the matter for Dalton.

'All right,' he said. He firmed his shoulders and turned towards the tent flap. 'We act.'

'What's your plan?'

Dalton thought quickly, noting their lack of weapons while considering how much weaponry Brady and Owen had between them. Then he remembered Houston standing alone, something he'd apparently done ever since most of his men had left town and not returned.

They'd never be able to help Kyle with strength,

84

but maybe if he'd understood the situation here correctly they had another option.

'Have you played much poker, Loren?' he asked.

'I used to,' Loren said.

Dalton put a hand on the flap and prepared to raise it.

'Then put on the kind of expression you'd have if you've just bet a thousand dollars you don't have on a bluff against a trigger-happy gunslinger. Then follow me out.'

CHAPTER 8

When Dalton pushed outside the scene was pretty much as he'd imagined it would be. Brady was walking away from him down the road while two men held either end of a taut rope in the middle of which was the captured Kyle.

Kyle was digging his heels in and fighting to avoid making every step, but he could do nothing to halt the two men who dragged him relentlessly on. Luckily, with all attention being on him, nobody noticed the two men emerging from the tent.

Dalton confirmed that Houston Floyd was still standing alone in the middle of the road. He set off towards him with Loren pacing along behind. They breezed past Owen, who cast a warning glare at them as if he'd already worked out their purpose, but they ignored him.

'Houston Floyd,' Dalton said in loud voice that made everyone on the road, including the departing Brady, look at him, 'I want a word with you.'

Houston glared at him while snorting his breath,

showing he was unaccustomed to being spoken to in this manner, but for his bluff to work, Dalton had to act arrogantly.

'Why would I want to speak to the likes of you?' Houston snapped.

Dalton didn't reply until he reached him letting him hear Brady muttering, presumably as he recognized Dalton.

'Because,' Dalton said lowering his voice, 'you're a fool who made a move on Cornelius Gash too early and now I'm your only hope.'

Houston's mouth fell open, betraying his shock and confirming that Dalton's hunch was right, before he got himself under control by running his gaze along the road to check nobody was close enough to hear them.

'Cornelius is my friend and ally,' he said, rocking his head to one side in a guarded manner. 'I'd never make a move on him.'

'I know the way it is. Cornelius at the mine, you here, and both wanting it all. You decided to chip away at Cornelius's position when he sent out that gold shipment, but he already had his suspicions. The men you sent to ambush it failed and now you're isolated and relying on Owen to maintain your precarious position.'

Houston flared his eyes, his face darkening, but Dalton had hoped to see that reaction.

'How do you know they failed?' he said.

'Because Cornelius hired us to make sure they did. Now they're all rotting back at the mine.'

87

Houston considered Dalton then Loren, taking in their grimed clothing and their lack of obvious weaponry.

'Perhaps you two got to know something about what happened to the shipment, but if it did get through after all, that had nothing to do with two men who I hear arrived in town on foot.'

'We don't look good right now,' Dalton said laughing as he looked down at his grimed clothing, 'but that'll change when you hire us.'

'Hire? After what you've just claimed?'

'Sure. We foiled your ambush and brought the gold back to the mine, but Cornelius double-crossed us and threw us in a cave. We escaped and now we want a new deal with you.'

Houston looked at each man in turn. He shook his head. For their part Dalton and Loren stood tall and tried to look as menacing as they could. Slowly Houston looked to one side as Brady came over.

'How did you two escape?' Brady murmured, his comment making Houston raise his eyebrows. 'The last I saw of you, that gate had closed and Cornelius was all set to throw away the key.'

'So they did escape,' Houston mused.

'Yeah, Cornelius threw them in a cave after they brought the gold back, but—'

'Enough!' Houston snapped. He paced up to Dalton. 'So some of your story might be true, after all. You two will come inside and give me the rest of your proposition.'

'Three,' Dalton said, then gestured towards the

bound Kyle.

Everyone looked at Kyle who for the first time looked up with hope brightening his eyes.

'Three it is.' Houston pointed at Brady. He gave a small gesture with his hand that directed him to untie Kyle. Then he turned on his heel in a quick manner that said he didn't expect any argument.

At first Brady didn't react other than to sneer, but as Houston continued to walk away he snapped out an order for his men to release Kyle.

'I don't know what you're trying to do here, Dalton,' he said as the men worked on Kyle's bonds, 'but stay out of my way.'

'A man who's only fit to run errands for Cornelius and Houston would do well to stay out of my way.' Dalton looked Brady up and down, sneering, then forced a laugh. 'I know about the third crate of gold. Breathe a word of what you've seen here and I'll tell Cornelius. You'll be dead before I finish speaking.'

'And that's the reason why I'll kill you.' Brady looked around, smirking, taking in Owen Muldoon over by the fallen tent. 'Houston may have chosen to use you and Owen may keep the peace here, but they only operate in Durando and there's a big world out there. You'll have to leave town one day and when that day comes I'll be waiting for you.'

With that threat made Brady backed away a slow pace. Then he turned on his heel and joined his men.

Dalton watched them head to their horses. Then he and Loren waited for Kyle to come over. For his part Kyle looked shamefaced as he stood alone, being unsure whom he could trust after the rapid change in the situation. Loren spoke up first.

'You'd better join us and see this through,' he said.

'I . . . I don't understand,' Kyle murmured, shuffling closer to them.

'There's nothing to understand. We saved your life, against our better judgement.'

'Then I'm obliged.'

'Then show it,' Dalton snapped, relieving some of the tension he felt. 'You've disappointed us twice. You won't get a third chance.'

Kyle sighed with relief. 'I'll do whatever you tell me to do.'

'Then stand behind us,' Dalton said, 'be quiet, and go along with everything we say.'

Then he headed to the saloon, hoping that Houston hadn't thought too much about their offer and uncovered its obvious flaws. But when they joined him he was in an amiable frame of mind.

Even better, Dalton had correctly deduced what had been happening here. A power struggle had been in progress ever since Cornelius had seized control of the mine from Perry Haynes, a struggle in which Cornelius and Houston were the main players and Brady and Owen were vying for position behind them.

This week Houston had grown weary of only controlling Durando and had moved in on Cornelius by sending his hired guns to ambush the gold shipment, but they had failed and now he was

90

vulnerable and desperate for help.

'If I accept your help,' he said when he'd accepted their credentials as hired guns willing to transfer allegiances, 'how much will it cost me?'

'Revenge is all we want,' Dalton said.

This surprised Houston. While he struggled to find an answer, Loren leaned over the table.

'Although Cornelius's kidnapped woman would keep us happy,' he said. 'After he double crossed us, we want her exclusively.'

'That's a simple matter,' Houston murmured with a wave of the hand, 'but even with your help I can't move on Cornelius again right now. The last attempt took a lot of planning and I still failed. My next move will be a long time coming.'

'It won't. Owen has plenty of men working for him and you can easily buy the few we'll need to take the mine.'

'Take the mine!' Houston spluttered. 'That's impossible. There's only one way in and it's well defended.'

'You're forgetting that we escaped from a cave that Cornelius thought was secure, and he doesn't even know we've gone.' Dalton leaned forward and smiled. 'We did it by finding a way out of the mine that he doesn't know about. And if we can get out unseen, we can get back in unseen.'

Houston looked aloft as he allowed this information to sink in, then joined Dalton in smiling.

'Sundown tomorrow, then.'

With that matter settled Loren and Kyle followed

Dalton off the dais. As they'd been seen talking with Houston, everyone moved out of their way giving them a dignified exit that helped to maintain their apparent status.

Only when they were heading back to the tent did they talk.

'That went better than I could have hoped for,' Dalton whispered.

'Sure,' Loren said. 'You almost had me believing we were guns for hire.'

Dalton laughed but Kyle shook his head.

'I'm mighty obliged you saved me,' he said, trotting along sideways to keep both men in his view, 'but I don't understand what you're doing. That sounded to me like you've found a way to get us killed real quick.'

'It probably is, but never forget that we only came up with this plan so that we could save your life and that means you'll back us no matter what we do.'

Kyle lowered his head looking suitably embarrassed for having complained.

When they reached the collapsed tent Loren stopped.

'I hate to say this,' he said, 'but Kyle's right. You did what you had to do back there, but I can't see how we can turn this round and get what we want: Perry Haynes being back in charge of the mine and his daughter being free.'

Dalton spread his hands. 'And in all honesty neither can I, but we have twenty-four hours to work out how.'

Loren smiled in appreciation of Dalton's honesty. They set off for the tent in which they'd left Mattie, but when Loren reached for the tent-flap, the flap to the next tent swung open and two men emerged.

Just as Dalton noted their familiar clothing, which he and Loren had been wearing an hour ago, Sheckley, the miner he'd taken Mattie away from, pushed his way out of their tent.

'I said there were plenty of dark tunnels back at the mine,' Sheckley said, bunching a fist, 'but I don't reckon you should wait that long to get what's coming to you.'

Dalton backed away but not for long as more miners emerged from the tents to form an unbroken circle around them. Each man was sneering and flexing his fists.

Worse, Owen Muldoon was nowhere to be seen and Dalton reckoned that after what he'd just done, he wouldn't help them anyhow.

CHAPTER 9

'We work for Houston now,' Loren said, 'so stand aside.'

This comment made Sheckley stop walking towards Dalton, but one look at how much help he had bolstered his courage and he set his stance belligerently with his hands on his hips.

'Houston ain't here now,' he said. 'We are.'

'And so is Owen Muldoon,' Dalton said, pacing up to join Loren. He set his jaw in a serious and confident manner despite not expecting help from that quarter. 'He won't stand for you beating on us.'

'Owen believes in justice. He'll know what you did to two of our friends earlier and that means he won't stop us.'

'You don't know what's at stake here. We're on your side.'

'You ain't on our side. You just arrived.' Sheckley advanced on him with a raised fist. 'I've been asking around and nobody recognizes you.'

'They should. We were at the mine earlier.' This

answer didn't stop the advancing miner. In desperation Dalton blurted out the one fact he hoped would provoke a reaction. 'We're friends of Perry Haynes.'

This only enraged Sheckley even more. With his face darkening he swung back his fist.

'You don't know Perry. He's long gone.'

Then he threw himself at Dalton, but Dalton had expected this action. He jerked to the side to avoid Sheckley's outstretched arms. Then he helped him on his way by swinging round and delivering a kick to the rump that sent him to the dirt. He turned ready to take on the next man only to find that the whole circle of miners had swarmed in at once and he was facing at least five men.

With no other choice open to him he stood back to back with Loren and took them on. He grounded the first man with a sharp uppercut to the chin, barged the second man to the ground with a flurry of jabs, but then they overwhelmed him as punches and kicks rained down on him from all directions.

He dodged and deflected many of the attacks, but there were too many of them. Blows to the kidneys came from behind and blows to the jaw came from the side. He'd have fallen but so many men were pressing against him they were holding him up.

Through the tangle of limbs and weaving bodies he caught glimpses of Loren and Kyle; they were faring as badly as he was. Kyle was lying pole-axed on the ground and being kicked and stamped on. Loren was being held up by two brawny men while three other men took it in turns to administer a steady rain of blows.

Somewhere Mattie was shouting at them to stop, but he took that as a good sign as it meant the miners weren't assaulting her.

Then a heavy blow to the cheek sent him reeling through his antagonists. When he collapsed to his knees he found himself in clear space. He jumped to his feet quickly, ready to get in a few blows of his own, but the sight of Owen Muldoon standing beside their tent caught his attention.

Owen was enjoying a smoke with two other men. When he saw Dalton, he gave him a cheery and mocking wave. Then two miners ran into Dalton and pushed him to the ground. He looked at the dirt, knowing that no help would come. Worse, he couldn't summon the strength to resist when he was dragged to his feet.

He was held upright to receive a punch to the jaw that cracked his head back, but he didn't fall as he staggered into a man who held him up, stood him straight then hit him again.

This time he saw that seven men had formed a circle around him. They proceeded to knock him from one man to the next, each getting in at least one blow before they passed him on.

As much as was possible Dalton rolled with the blows, hoping they'd deem themselves to have had enough before he passed out. He'd been round them all and was starting on a second round when Owen's strident voice barked out.

'That's enough,' he roared.

Dalton's current assailant was Sheckley. He looked to the side to see Owen advancing on him, then he thundered another low blow into Dalton's guts.

'We're just settling something,' he said, 'that didn't interest you.'

'It did, but I knew what they'd done, so I left it to you to end this.' Owen raised his eyebrows, inviting a response.

For long moments Dalton thought the miners wouldn't take up his offer to desist, but when Owen's men joined him, Sheckley raised his hands.

'Yeah. We got what we came for.' He pointed at Dalton. 'So stay out of those dark tunnels if you enjoy being alive.'

'I can't do that,' Dalton gasped, deciding that despite the situation he'd test out an idea. 'No matter how bad the wages, a man has to work.'

'He does, and that's the lesson you need to learn. When the likes of Cornelius Gash increase hours, cut back wages and treat us like dirt, we have to stick together. Anyone who turns on a fellow miner ain't welcome no longer.'

Dalton considered him and despite the pain this man had inflicted he saw that he had done it through loyalty. This gave further weight to his idea, but before he could continue testing his theory, Sheckley gestured for the men holding him up to release him.

Despite the warning Dalton's legs gave way and he tumbled to the ground. He lay, watching Kyle and Loren being released from their own particular torment. Each man stumbled. Kyle fell like a chopped-down tree while Loren managed to throw out a leg to stop himself falling, although he then stood stooped and bloodied.

As the miners backed away, each snorting with derision as they passed them to head towards the saloon, Mattie checked on each of them. Both Loren and Dalton told her to help Kyle first.

Owen watched her, sneering. Then he headed over to Dalton. By the time he reached him Dalton had levered himself off the ground.

'You three ain't no hired guns!' Owen snorted.

Sudden anger flared in Dalton's mind. He leaned to the side to spit out a mouthful of bloody saliva, then paced up to Owen.

'I've done things that'd shock even you. Don't doubt me again.'

'Hey,' Owen said, backing away a pace although a smile was hovering on his lips, 'I sure didn't mean to criticize a man who's just been beaten to a pulp. I wish you a whole heap of luck in your futile mission to break into the mine and get Houston killed.'

Dalton pointed at him. 'Don't be so sure that'll happen.'

'I'm counting on it.' Owen chuckled. 'Why else do you think I stepped in and saved you?'

Owen then turned on his heel and gestured for his men to join him in heading back to the saloon.

Fifteen minutes later Dalton, Loren and Kyle were sitting in a tent while Mattie moved from one man to the next bathing wounds. Aside from bruising, each man had come out of his ordeal without any serious or permanent injury. Although how stiff they would be tomorrow was something Dalton didn't like to think about.

'What did you take from what Owen said?' Loren asked.

'Same as you,' Dalton said. 'Like everybody else, Owen wants to take over his own slice of territory.'

'And then somebody will come along and take it away from him.' Loren sighed. 'I sure hate this place and once we get back to Two Forks I ain't ever leaving again.'

'That much is certain,' Dalton said, although right now he had grave worries he'd ever get to see his home and wife again.

'And one other thing is certain: Perry was wrong about Owen.'

Dalton shrugged. 'Perhaps he was, but I'm not sure Owen's motives are as base as everyone else's are. He still knows right from wrong and he's doing the best he can here.'

'Then I ain't the only one who can be more forgiving than is natural.' Loren blew out his cheeks then glanced at Kyle, who was lying on the blanket, gingerly rubbing his ribs. 'But whatever is on Owen's mind, he fought on our side.'

'Once,' Dalton snapped, surprising himself with his anger. He stared at Kyle until he looked at him. 'You've proved yourself once, but you let us down twice. You need to prove yourself again before we'll trust you and another time after that before we'll let you return with us to Two Forks.'

'I intend to do just that,' Kyle said, his voice sounding serious and determined, 'if you'll include me in your plans.'

Dalton looked at Loren and winked. 'I guess to do that we need to have a plan in the first place.'

When Dalton awoke he was surprised to find it was light. More surprisingly, when he poked his head out of the tent to consider the deserted town the sun was beating down from high in the sky.

Back in Two Forks he always woke at first light, but last night sleep had been a long time coming as he received proof that Durando was a town that only came alive after sundown.

The revelries had continued long into the night with frequent comings and goings, all noisy and distracting, taking place in the tents around them, making the difficult task of having four people sleep together in a small tent even harder. This was especially so with one of their number being a woman and with the men all groaning every time they moved and located a new bruise.

Outside the saloon two fist fights had erupted, which had required Owen's intervention. Later a third fight had descended into gunfire that resulted in one man being run out of town and the other being taken away feet first. This appeared to dampen everyone's spirits and for the rest of the night the town had become quieter.

Watching these altercations in which he wasn't

involved helped to confirm Dalton's belief about Owen's attitude. Accordingly, he wasn't disappointed when, after they'd been awake for an hour, Owen visited them. He threw three gunbelts into the tent then cast a surly glare around.

'She's coming with me,' he informed them, pointing at Mattie.

'She ain't going nowhere,' Loren snapped.

'She is. While you're getting your stupid hides shot to pieces tonight, Houston wants me to make sure she doesn't run.' Owen looked at each man in turn. 'Or gets help from someone to run.'

Everybody kept their expressions blank in case Owen's comment hadn't had a sinister intent.

'Take special care she comes to no harm then,' Loren said, 'for when we come back.'

Owen shrugged. 'You won't be coming back.'

'We will,' Dalton said, 'with your help.'

This comment took Owen aback and, as Dalton hadn't discussed his intentions with anyone else, Loren raised his eyebrows while Kyle and Mattie both murmured something to themselves.

'Help?' Owen spluttered. He waited for a response but when Dalton stayed quiet, he set his hands on his hips. 'My only interest is in satisfying the men who pay me, a job that'll be harder if Houston manages to buy my men.'

'You can find more.'

'Not easily. It took me months to train them and now Houston will get them killed.' Owen shook his head. 'Either way, I ain't helping three fools who are pretending to be gunslingers.'

'We aren't fools.' Dalton lowered his voice. 'But you're right that we aren't gunslingers. We intend to free Perry Haynes and restore him as the mine owner. To do that we'll have to get rid of Cornelius, Brady and Houston. Then, when Perry is running the mine again, you'll look after Durando.'

For a minute silence reigned. Then, with a glance outside, Owen closed the flaps behind him and joined them in the crowded tent. He stood in the centre and considered them all in turn until he stopped, facing Dalton.

'Only a fool would make that claim, but as you say you're not one, why did you tell me that?'

'It was a show of faith that you'll repay when you help us make Durando and the mine run the way you know they should be run.'

Owen's prolonged silence implied he was giving Dalton's comment serious consideration before he hunkered down to meet his gaze.

'You've misjudged me.'

'I haven't. In a town with a proper system of authority you'd be the man everyone would want as town marshal. Maybe you even will be soon and then you can start to build something here that'll work.'

'Durando is a festering boil and soon that boil will get lanced and fade away.' Owen pointed towards the mine. 'Men come here for one reason only and as soon as that's gone, they'll be gone, too. There ain't no point building anything here.'

Dalton leaned forward. 'You're wrong. The DMC

is no prospector's gold rush that bleeds out in a year. The mine could outlast us all, which means people will view this place as home. And then they'll realize this is a mighty fine area with plenty to offer a man beyond gold.'

Owen rocked back on his heels snorting and waving in a dismissive manner at Dalton.

'You really are a fool. Nobody sees this place as home, only as a living hell.'

'They do now with Cornelius running the mine, but they didn't when Perry Haynes was in charge. He dealt with men fairly and that meant the miners weren't so edgy. When he's in charge again, life in Durando will become tolerable.'

Owen didn't reply immediately, confirming that in this, Dalton had been right.

'What are you asking of me, Dalton?'

'I'm asking for your help and you'll give it because you know it's the right thing to do. This is the one chance you have of making this town run the proper way by removing those who want power for selfish reasons.'

'Noble aims, Dalton,' Owen said, shaking his head as he pulled Mattie to her feet, 'but you've got the wrong man.'

Loren gave Mattie a quick nod to say she would be fine. Dalton looked at Owen.

'I haven't,' he said, halting him with a hand holding the flap high.

Owen stayed looking outside, shaking his head. Then, without further comment, he pushed Mattie outside and headed off, leaving everyone in the tent to look at Dalton.

'I hope you're not pinning all your hopes on that man,' Loren said, 'because he didn't want to hear what you had to say.'

'Except he heard me out,' Dalton said. 'So I hope that means he really is the man Durando needs.'

CHAPTER 10

It was mid-afternoon when a combination of thirst, boredom and stiffness forced Dalton, Loren and Kyle to slip out of their tent.

Within seconds, they regretted leaving.

On the opposite side of the thoroughfare three men were idly chatting amongst themselves, but they stopped talking to watch them. Dalton recognized one of the men as Dagwood Brent, one of the group who had searched for Kyle yesterday. He leaned towards Loren and he confirmed that the other two had also been with Brady yesterday.

Brady's men watched them with lively grins on their faces. The moment Dalton and the other two moved off they sauntered towards them. Dalton kept his gaze set on the saloon, watching the men from the corner of his eye, but they kept moving slowly, making no effort to intercept them and merely ensuring that they'd been noticed.

'Waiting for us to leave town?' Dalton asked when they reached the saloon door.

'Or looking for an opportunity to get us out of town,' Loren said.

'Then they'll fail. I don't intend to leave the saloon until I've drunk my weight in coffee.'

Loren smiled and pushed through the doors.

This early in the day the saloon was almost empty. Owen and a few of his men were sitting on the dais. Houston Floyd was again sitting on his own at the opposite end. Worryingly, both men looked at them without acknowledging them, and when Dalton heard the doors swing open behind him as Brady's men entered, a nervous tremor fluttered in his guts.

He put his worries from his mind and, with Loren and Kyle, he headed to the bar and ordered three coffees. When the coffee arrived the three men hunched over their mugs while the bartender headed down the bar to deal with Brady's men.

'I wonder where Mattie is,' Loren said.

'She'll be safe,' Dalton said. 'Houston wouldn't want such a valuable person to get hurt.'

Loren winced. 'She sure is valuable.'

Dalton smiled. His friend rarely showed an interest in women, but now that he thought about it, Loren had found plenty of excuses to sit with her this morning and he had been quiet since Owen took her away.

He was about to rib him about his feelings for her when he heard Dagwood mutter his name, closely followed by a snort of laughter. Then a full whiskey glass came skidding down the bar, a sticky patch making it come to a sudden halt and splash whiskey

106

over his right hand.

He considered the glass then picked it up and turned.

'Obliged,' he said, raising the glass in a silent salute to Dagwood. 'Maybe if you're staying I'll buy you one in return.'

Dagwood glanced at the other two men and smirked, clearly pleased that his attempt to force a confrontation had worked. He walked down the bar to join Dalton. The other two men swung round to watch what might take place.

'I ain't staying.' Dagwood smiled. 'And neither are you.'

'We'll leave when we choose to. That might be now, tomorrow, or never.'

Dagwood's sneer suggested that he didn't know they would be attempting an assault on the mine tonight.

'It won't be never. You'll leave, one way or the other, and when you do, Brady will be waiting for you.'

'I'm looking forward to it, but I'll deal with him at a time of my choosing.'

With that comment Dalton placed the whiskey glass back on the bar without taking a drink. He picked up his coffee mug.

'You won't be able to stay close to Owen for ever,' Dagwood said. 'The first moment you leave his sight will be your last.'

Dagwood barked a laugh, then sauntered back down the bar to join the other men. Dalton leaned on the bar beside Loren.

'At least,' Loren whispered, 'that confirms what they intend to do. We must hope that now that they've warned us they'll go back to the mine, because if they stay they're sure to find out what we're planning.'

'Agreed. They. . . .' Dalton trailed off when he heard footfalls. He looked towards the dais to see that Houston was approaching. When he reached them, Dalton nodded towards the end of the bar. 'They're Brady's men, Houston, and they're watching everything we do.'

'That doesn't matter,' Houston said. 'We won't be going anywhere tonight. We only have four men who are prepared to attack the mine.'

'Four!' Dalton spluttered, then lowered his voice in case Dagwood overheard him. 'You must be able to get more than that.'

Houston snorted a laugh. 'Before you start worrying about that, you need to ask who those four are.'

Dalton considered Houston's sneering glare. He sighed as he grasped his meaning.

'Would those four include you?'

'Yup.'

'And me?'

'And Loren, and this one.' Houston pointed at Kyle. 'After the beating you got last night, nobody is prepared to risk their lives following you, no matter what I offer.'

Dalton winced. He glanced up at the men on the dais. Several of them chose that moment to sneer.

'Twenty men against three. We couldn't do nothing about that.'

'Maybe not, but would you follow a man who couldn't find a way to fight back?'

Houston gave Dalton a significant look. Then he turned on his heel and headed back to his position on the dais.

For several minutes the three men didn't speak. Kyle stayed hunched over his coffee. Dalton judged he was avoiding catching anyone's eye now that the plan, which in his view would just get them all killed, was doomed. Loren tensed his jaw as he pondered. Then he turned to Dalton.

'He's right. We don't exactly look and act like guns for hire. I wouldn't follow us.'

'Agreed. So maybe now is the time we start fighting back.'

Dalton took a look slurp of his coffee, then slammed it down on the bar. He turned to Dagwood.

The three men had been watching the discussion with Houston with interest, even if they hadn't been able to hear what it was about.

Dalton picked up the whiskey glass; then with it held high between two fingers he paced down the bar. Dagwood pushed himself away from the bar and eyed his approach with a surly smile on his lips.

Dalton stopped in front of him, looked Dagwood up and down, then, while meeting his eye, he poured the whiskey over his boots. Dagwood kept smiling as he shuffled from side to side, spreading the pool of whiskey.

'Now why did you go and do that?' he asked.

'Because I've made a decision. I ain't waiting for you to jump us and drag us out of town to face Brady. You're taking a message to him.'

'I ain't no messenger.'

'It ain't that kind of message.' Dalton opened his fingers, letting the glass drop, but before it hit the floor he followed through with a short-armed punch that hit Dagwood squarely on the nose.

The blow came from close to and landed without much force, but the pain was enough to send Dagwood staggering backwards for a pace. Dalton didn't give him a chance to recover. He followed through with an uppercut to his chin with one fist that stood him straight and a low blow to the belly with the other that had Dagwood folding over, coughing.

The other two men hurried down the bar and squared up to Loren and Kyle. From the corner of his eye Dalton was pleased to see that when the opposition was more evenly matched his colleagues fared better.

Loren delivered a rapid flurry of blows to his assailant that rocked him back against the bar where he stood trapped and unable to avoid the blows that came from the left and right. Even Kyle got the better of his opponent and floored him with a round-arm punch to the cheek.

Heartened now, Dalton waited until Dagwood straightened. Then he put all his pent-up frustration of the last day into a swinging punch that connected with Dagwood's jaw and sent him reeling. As Dalton wrung his hand Dagwood slid across the floor until his head slammed into the base of the wall with a thud that made him go limp.

Dalton turned to see that Loren had already floored his opponent and was moving to help Kyle, but before he reached him Kyle sent his assailant spinning over the bar to clatter to the floor on the other side. Then Kyle patted his hands together and with Loren turned to smile at him.

Dalton acknowledged them with a nod, then looked at Houston. He hadn't changed his stern expression so Dalton couldn't tell whether bettering Brady's men had changed his opinion of them, but he figured they'd done everything they could. The rest was up to Owen's men.

He joined Loren and Kyle, aiming to finish his coffee, but as he reached for his mug, Kyle's mouth fell open in shock. His finger rose to point past his shoulder.

'Watch out!' he shouted.

Dalton turned at the hip, his gun coming to hand. Kyle's warning let him pick out Dagwood as he raised himself with his gun drawn and aimed at him.

With no choice Dalton fired. His slug slammed high into Dagwood's chest and knocked him back into the wall. Dagwood's shot wasted itself into the floor. His gun fell from his slack fingers, but Dalton kept his gun on him as he watched him twitch, then slump to lie on the floor.

Loren also drew his gun and kept it on the man

he'd knocked out, while Kyle drew his gun before he glanced over the bar at his assailant.

Dalton heard men getting to their feet on the dais and in several long paces Owen joined them. He gave Dalton a quick glance, then breezed past him to stand over Dagwood's body.

'Get these varmints out of town,' he said, gesturing to his men, 'and from now on Brady and anyone associated with him ain't welcome in Durando.'

Men hurried to comply with his wishes. Owen helped them to remove the body and the comatose men. Throughout he didn't catch Dalton's eye again.

When Owen had gone, Dalton nodded to Kyle.

'Obliged,' he said.

'I said you could trust me,' Kyle said.

'That's twice you've proved that. Now we're even. Prove yourself one more time and you'll get to return to Two Forks with our blessing.'

Kyle rolled his shoulders, his stance suggesting he was determined to do just that.

Dalton watched him, still unable to dismiss the images of him running away having stolen the gold, or to forget the knock on the head, but Loren distracted him when he pointed out that Houston was making for the bar.

Houston nodded to them, then leaned back against the bar and looked at the men on the dais. They hadn't joined Owen in dealing with Brady's men. Several of them met his eye. Then one man stood and made his way to the bar.

The man shuffled from foot to foot, then took a deep breath.

'Does your offer still stand?' he asked.

CHAPTER 11

As arranged, they left town at sundown.

Dalton, Loren and Kyle joined Houston's group of the six hired guns whom he had persuaded to join them. Without comment they slotted in behind the wagon carrying the equipment they'd need for the operation. As they headed to the mine they rode stiffly in the saddle, every bruise repeatedly reminding them of its presence.

They took a detour in case Brady was scouting around, but without incident they reached the point where the trail veered down to Two Forks. This was the place where only yesterday they had embarked on what they had hoped would be the final leg of their journey to deliver the gold.

That day now felt like it was an age ago.

'You'll lead from here,' Houston said, gesturing ahead for Dalton to ride up front.

'Sure,' Dalton said. 'Nobody was on guard when we escaped yesterday, but in case anybody is around tonight, be quiet and go slowly. We have plenty of time before the moon rises.'

'Understood,' Houston said; then he beckoned for Dalton to lead on.

Although the sun had set an hour ago, there was still enough afterglow in the summer sky for Dalton to find the route to the mine easily.

When they reached the ridge at the back end of the mine encampment he looked along its length for guards. As the steep and often overhanging ridge provided a natural barrier to anyone seeking a way into the encampment, he saw nobody on lookout. He gestured for everyone to follow him and, at a steady pace, they rode along with Dalton peering ahead into the gloom.

As they closed on the area where they'd climbed out of the hole yesterday Dalton slowed, as he didn't want to risk falling into the pit. When he saw the winch, he gestured for Loren to dismount and check ahead.

Loren edged forward until he reached a patch of inky darkness in the ground. He looked at it cautiously before turning and nodding.

'We've found it, Houston,' he called out, his voice echoing beneath the overhang.

Dalton swung round in the saddle.

'Houston!' he said, his voice also echoing. 'We've found it.'

'I heard,' Houston grunted, 'and be quiet or everyone in the encampment will know we've found it too.'

Loren threw a stone into the pit and listened to it

clatter below. Then he turned.

'It's as we remembered it, Houston,' he said, this time lowering his voice so that it didn't echo. 'We'll have no trouble getting you into the encampment to take on Cornelius.'

Houston jumped down from his horse. He hurried over to Loren, a finger to his lips and his bemusement at Loren's behaviour clear even in the poor light. So, from behind him, Dalton flashed Loren a warning glare that said he'd mentioned they had Houston with them enough times now to alert Perry down in the pit.

Loren said nothing more. Houston gestured for his men to join him. They debated how they'd proceed, many taking the opportunity to look into the dark hole and mutter unhappily, so Houston ordered one of them to light a brand and throw it down.

Before anyone reacted Dalton hurried to the wagon carrying the brands, poles and other equipment. He took as much time as he could without drawing suspicion on himself to light a brand, which he threw into the pit.

He breathed a sigh of relief when he saw that Perry wasn't there. Then, in short order, strong rope was attached to the abandoned winch and dropped down. Dalton grabbed the rope, not letting anyone else get down first, then lowered himself into the hole to reach the ledge.

He then found that getting off the ledge to reach the wall was tricky. So he told those above to go all the way to the bottom in one go, making sure he mentioned Houston a few times in the process.

Then he kicked the brand the rest of the way to the bottom of the pit and took the rope. He lowered himself beneath the ledge and swung out beneath it. A glance around confirmed that Perry wasn't there.

When he reached the bottom he found that he was effectively in a tunnel. His quick look along it confirmed that it went in a straight direction for fifty yards before swinging to the right.

Luckily this was how he'd envisaged the terrain when he'd been in the dark, so he hoped that his memory continued to be this good.

Loren climbed down next.

'Perry took the hint, thankfully,' he whispered.

'Let's hope he trusts us enough to understand why we've done this and doesn't think we've double-crossed him.'

'Until we meet him we won't know that for sure, but either way, that's one big problem down, another big one to come.'

Dalton winced. 'Don't worry. I committed the route to memory. I can get us in.'

'You'd better hope you can because remember what Perry said. We could roam around under here for days and never find our way out.'

Dalton started to offer further assurance that made light of his own concern, but then silenced when the first man to climb down into the pit arrived. So, while leaning back against the tunnel wall and trying to look unconcerned, they watched

117

their temporary colleagues' progress.

Two other men came down, then Houston. Then the tricky task of manoeuvring the long poles down followed. Kyle was the last to join them and he volunteered to bring up the rear.

They set off down the tunnel with Dalton leading the way and Loren close behind. Dalton had a clear view of the route ahead and although, unlike on their previous journey, there was no danger of his knocking himself against the walls and roof he maintained a slow pace. This gave him time to think about the route ahead.

When he reached the section of the tunnel where it turned sharply to the right he crossed his fingers for the first time. He'd remembered that ahead they'd walked through an airy-feeling section. Sure enough, he found himself in a cave that was so vast the light from their brands barely lit the roof.

Houston called for more light. This helped to light up the area and let Dalton see that there was a tunnel on the opposite side of the cave, as he'd remembered. Despite this confidence boost he continued to walk slowly.

'Hurry up,' Houston muttered, inevitably.

'We'll keep going slowly and you need to be quiet,' Dalton said. 'Noise can make walls collapse and then we'll never get out.'

Dalton didn't know whether this was true but it silenced Houston. So, feeling in a relaxed frame of mind for the first time, Dalton entered the tunnel and headed down it. His recollection was that after twenty paces there had been a narrow stretch where they'd crawled through one at a time.

Sure enough the tunnel closed down to a thin and wet horizontal slice cut through the rock, presumably an area where water had eroded a softer rock seam.

Dalton gave everyone guidance and warnings to ensure they went through slowly, again to give him time to think through what he expected to find in the next section. Then, on his belly, he went through the seam first.

He was disappointed to find that the slice through the rock was wide and easy to negotiate. He'd envisaged it as a thin and difficult to climb through tunnel with the sides being close. His discomfort grew when he reached the other side and faced a decision he hadn't expected.

The cave into which he had climbed had four exits, of different sizes, each going off in a different direction.

He ran through his memory of this section of their journey, but at the time, coming from the other direction, he hadn't been aware of the four different routes. They had just carried straight on then ducked to enter the seam.

This meant it was likely that one of the two tunnels ahead was the one to take, but he didn't know which one and he was no nearer to a decision when Loren joined him.

'Stay here, Loren,' he said, pointing at the left-hand tunnel. 'I'll investigate this one.'

Loren narrowed his eyes, clearly noting Dalton's concern, but said nothing.

Dalton hurried off, covering thirty yards of tunnel quickly. After that he found himself in a large cave where water roared as it rushed by somewhere close by. When he thought back he recalled that he had heard water at this stage, although he'd remembered it as being not so noisy. His discomfort increased when he saw that the cave was riddled with holes.

He counted twenty before he gave up counting and started to look into each. Some went on for only yards but others carried on for longer than his brand would light.

He thought back to this part of the journey but all he could remember was water running beside him and a steady forward motion. That suggested he should try one of the tunnels ahead, but even then there were five from which to choose.

The first tremor of panic at being lost underground battered at his thoughts but he fought the feeling away. There had to be a way to work out which direction was the right one without letting on to Houston that he didn't know which way to go, but he couldn't think what. Then Loren shouted down the tunnel.

'You won't find a quicker way, Dalton,' he said. 'Come back.'

There had been a second promising tunnel in the smaller cave, but Loren hadn't paid attention to their route when they'd escaped, so it was unlikely he had worked out that it was the right way to go. So this comment bemused him but he didn't dare ask what it meant in case it alerted Houston.

Feeling despondent, Dalton made his way back to find that most of the men had made it through the seam and were in the midst of performing the tricky manoeuvre of pushing the poles through the gap. Dalton stayed out of their way and joined Loren.

He frowned, but to his surprise Loren winked, then nodded towards the right-hand tunnel, inviting Dalton to join him.

'We should get there soon,' Loren said, speaking loudly so that Houston would hear them and know they weren't sharing secrets.

'Glad to hear you're confident,' Dalton said, guardedly.

'Sure am. Just walk slowly and keep your eyes on the ground.'

Loren looked down. Dalton followed his gaze and saw that he was holding a scrap of cloth. Loren waited until Dalton had seen it, then dropped it to the ground and stood on it.

'Perry?' Dalton mouthed. He received a nod.

Dalton murmured his thanks then leaned back against the tunnel wall to wait for Houston to be ready.

When the poles were through he set off down the tunnel. The running water sounded less noisy: as he'd remembered it. His brand lit the straight path ahead and showed that he wouldn't face any tricky decisions for a while.

Confident now, he maintained a slow pace while

repeatedly looking at the ground, searching for more scraps of cloth but, just as he'd remembered it, the next hundred yards didn't present him with any choices.

Eventually they came out into a large circular cave, this being the place where Dalton had started to commit their path to memory. Accordingly, he turned to pace around the edge of the cave. Two paces on he found a scrap of cloth, which he kicked into the dirt. Five yards on he saw a second scrap lying beside a thin opening in the wall that he'd have missed without the clue.

This proved to be the area where the walls closed in so tightly that he had to walk sideways. With the tunnel being thin and veering to the right in a long curve, his followers struggled to push the poles along.

Loren stayed back to help them, leaving Dalton to hurry on ahead to ensure he picked up the remaining clues on the route he should take, but when he emerged into the next open space numerous possible exits faced him.

Each hole was small and hard to get through, and he couldn't find cloth beside any of them. He turned on the spot, trying to remember this section of the journey and failing to bring any thoughts to mind.

He was embarking on searching each exit again when, with a rueful smile to himself, he looked up.

The roof was ten feet above his head and in its centre was a rough circle marking the rock that capped what was to have been their prison.

He murmured a sigh of relief. He went to each of the exits and whispered for Perry, hoping he was close and that he'd be able to relay their plans, but he got no response. So he waited for everyone to join him then pointed upwards.

'Be quiet,' he whispered. 'We're in the mine encampment.'

'Well done,' Houston said, slapping his back.

Then he set about helping with the process of removing the capping rock. This proved to be easier than Dalton had expected. It would have been impossible for an unaided man to remove it even if he could get up there, but two strapped-together poles easily slid it to the side to reveal a slice of the night sky.

Quickly they extinguished their brands. Dalton split the poles and, using the strapping that held them together as a makeshift ladder, he clambered up to the surface and looked out. Nobody was in the hollow, so he rolled out on to the ground, then crawled to the edge of the hollow to look down the hill.

Everything was as he'd remembered it from yesterday. Situated beyond the bottom of the hill and across a hundred yards of open ground was the encampment where the miners rested. A smaller and neater encampment where presumably Cornelius and his guards stayed was set fifty yards away.

Aside from a few miners making their way from the main tunnel to the tents, nobody was outside other than the two guards at the mine entrance, and they were looking down the pass.

When Houston joined him he also took in the lay of the land, murmuring contentedly to himself.

'Provided we can find Cornelius quickly,' Dalton whispered when everyone had climbed out of the pit, 'we should be able to seize control without trouble.'

'Agreed,' Houston said. 'Any idea which tent is Cornelius's?'

'No.' Dalton ran his gaze over the tents, but didn't see any that were bigger than the rest. 'And I wouldn't like to guess.'

'That's fine. You got us this far and that's all you promised.' Houston pointed down the slope, signifying the route they would take. 'We get closer to the tents, take up positions, then raise a disturbance. When Cornelius comes out, we kill him. What happens then depends on how much loyalty his men have for a dead leader.'

Although Dalton balked at the first part of the plan, he had pinned his own hopes on the second. He didn't want to be involved in a bloodbath, but he hoped that removing the snake's head would end this assault quickly, after which they'd have to find a way to do the same to Houston.

The message about the route was still being passed around when over by the entrance the guards started moving. Then one guard hollered something that Dalton couldn't hear.

Dalton told everyone to be quiet, then he pointed at the entrance.

Everyone watched as the guard continued to

holler while walking towards the tents. Although his words weren't clear, his tone sounded as if he wanted help. The second guard stayed back and, in the poor light, Dalton was sure another man was now with him.

'Pity we aren't down there already,' he said. 'It sounds as if we're getting that disruption we wanted.'

Houston grunted that he agreed as several men emerged from the tents, Cornelius being amongst them. This group approached the guard, who pointed towards the hill. As one the men turned. Every one of them looked at the hollow where Dalton and the others were hiding.

Nobody moved, trusting that the darkness would keep them hidden.

'How did they work that out?' Houston murmured. 'We were quiet.'

'We were,' Dalton murmured.

He looked at the two men by the entrance and an unwelcome thought tapped at his mind. Then one of the men moved into a patch of light and the unwelcome thought became reality.

Wincing he looked down the line of men in the hollow. Excluding himself there were eight men: Loren, Houston, and the six men Houston had hired.

Kyle wasn't there; he was down by the entrance.

'That's Kyle!' Loren muttered beside him, noting what Dalton had seen. 'The double-crossing swine.'

Dalton thought back and recalled that he hadn't seen Kyle for some time. After volunteering to bring up the rear when they'd set off, he must have doubled back, climbed out of the hole, and issued the warning.

'Kyle is a dead man,' he muttered.

'You'll get no arguments from me this time,' Loren said.

Dalton swung round to explain to Houston what had happened, but it was to face a drawn gun aimed at his forehead.

'You have ten seconds to convince me he's working alone,' Houston said, 'or I'll blast you both to hell.'

CHAPTER 12

'Kyle's turned on us too,' Loren murmured, raising his hands as everyone followed Houston's lead and drew guns on them.

'You've used up two of your last ten seconds,' Houston said, 'and I ain't convinced yet.'

'We can't convince you of anything,' Dalton said. 'This is all our fault.'

'That was a brave thing to say! I'll take those as your last words.'

'Don't!' Dalton spluttered, raising a hand. 'I meant we should never have trusted Kyle. When we returned the gold he tried to steal it. Then when I helped Brady get it back, Brady stole some of it for himself. He tried to kill Kyle to silence him, so I stood up for Kyle and saved him. That was my mistake.'

'It sure was.' Houston firmed his gun hand, looking for a moment as if he'd fire, but then he raised his hand. 'But I believe you.'

'Obliged,' Dalton murmured in relief.

'Don't be. If I thought I could survive without you,

I'd have blasted you away. Now get me out of this.'

Dalton considered the situation, then pointed at the hole in the centre of the hollow.

'That's the only way.'

Houston shook his head. 'They can block us in at both ends. We stay out in the open.'

Dalton agreed with this sentiment. He looked down the slope, watching as Cornelius gathered men around him, then walked towards the hill. He noted that Brady was amongst the group, with Kyle and the guard from the entrance trailing along behind.

By the time Cornelius was fifty yards from the base of the hill he had gathered thirty men, outnumbering their group by more than three to one.

Brady slowed to let Cornelius get ahead before stopping to view the situation. Dalton noted his darting head movements as he picked out the men who had helped him track down Kyle. Although acting shiftily was probably normal for Brady, Dalton judged that he was planning something, and Dalton reckoned he knew what that was.

'I got me an idea,' he said to Houston.

'Then try it,' Houston said. 'But do it quickly. I'm shooting the moment Cornelius gets close enough.'

Dalton nodded. He raised himself so that he could be seen from below.

'Cornelius!' he shouted. 'It's Dalton.'

'I know,' Cornelius snapped. He halted while he was still out of range from the hollow. 'Kyle told me what you've done. I should never have believed a

128

word you said.'

'We all tell lies,' Dalton said. 'The trouble is, you haven't figured out who is telling you the biggest lies.'

'I know who that man is. Houston is up there too, and he must be more desperate than I thought to use you.'

'I don't mean Houston. I mean Brady Cox.'

This comment made Brady flinch and look around, his furtive gaze picking out several men, who eased away from the rest of the group, but they all stopped when Cornelius swirled round.

'Come here, Brady,' he said, 'and we'll get Dalton and Houston together.'

Brady shifted from foot to foot then shook his head.

'I'll stay here,' he said, 'until I know you ain't listening to him.'

Cornelius looked at him until he was sure he wouldn't move, then looked up towards the hollow.

'Say what's on your mind, Dalton. Then we'll kill you.'

'Houston tried to ambush your gold shipment, as you thought, and I brought it back. Except that Brady kept a crate for himself, and the only people who know that are up here and down there behind you.'

'Liar!' Brady shouted.

Brady looked around. His gaze picked out Kyle, who edged back a pace, then took another before he decided not to wait to see how the situation developed. He ran for the tents.

Kyle managed only ten paces before Brady drew his gun and blasted him in the back. Kyle staggered on for another pace but a second shot sent him to the dirt.

'Obliged, Brady,' Dalton shouted. 'That saved us the trouble. Now the only people who know about the gold you stole are up here.'

Dalton didn't know whether Brady would react to his taunt and risk an anger-fuelled assault on their position, but he got the better reaction when Cornelius roared with anger.

'You made a big mistake, Brady,' he shouted, 'when you stole off me.'

Brady swung back to face Cornelius, the determined stances of both men making those who had been standing between them scurry away to let them see each other directly.

'It ain't that simple, Cornelius,' Brady said.

'I don't need to hear no excuses. I just want my missing gold. Bring it here now or die.'

Brady considered Cornelius, his steady rocking motion from foot to foot conveying that he was weighing up his chances. And he could see what Dalton could see. He stood on open ground while Cornelius was standing near to the mine entrance, where there were numerous isolated rocks behind which he could seek cover.

Dalton reckoned Brady would relent, but with a great roar he threw himself to the side.

'Get him!' he shouted as he hit the ground and rolled.

130

For a frozen moment nobody moved as each person looked at the others, gauging what their reactions would be. Then two people close to Brady made their choice and hurried towards him while keeping everyone else in view. That helped the rest to decide where their loyalties should lie.

To Dalton's surprise most of them sided with Brady.

A wave of men backed away towards Brady. Then, on seeing that they were in the majority, they stopped and faced the smaller group. A few of these men hurried aside with their hands raised showing that they were abandoning Cornelius.

Then the shooting started.

Three of the men who had stayed with Cornelius went down in the initial onslaught, after which Cornelius took flight to hide out of Dalton's view in the mine entrance. Six men stayed with him and beat a retreat into hiding.

Despite their superior numbers Brady's group were on open ground. They ran towards the hill to seek cover. As they hurried away from the entrance Cornelius's group took out two men, and to add confusion Houston fired at them before they disappeared from sight at the bottom of the hill.

Then the serious shooting began, with rapid gunfire blasting out across the mine, but with all of it taking place out of view, Houston's group could do nothing but wait.

'Good work, Dalton,' Houston said. 'You set one man off against the other. Now all we have to do is dispose of whoever survives.'

Dalton nodded, avoiding giving any indication that this comment summed up his and Loren's plan for how they would put Perry back in charge.

'Sure,' he said. 'Let's hope that they fight this out for some time.'

Houston grunted that he agreed. Then they listened to the gunfight raging out of their sight at the bottom of the hill, while trying to deduce what was happening from the taunts and shouted demands.

'Give up,' Brady shouted.

'Never,' Cornelius countered.

Gunfire blasted for several minutes.

'You can still walk out of this alive. Just leave the mine to me.'

'I own this mine now. You work for me.'

'That's what Perry said.'

More gunfire erupted. Then a pained shout tore out followed by hollering for the shooting to stop. Slowly it petered out.

'We're coming out now,' someone shouted. Dalton didn't recognize the voice although he recognized the desperation in the tone. 'Don't shoot. We've had enough.'

'Then throw out your guns.'

Houston looked at Dalton. 'You reckon it's ended?'

Dalton nodded. 'I think they got Cornelius, so the rest have gone over to Brady.'

'Then get ready for an assault. It'll come any moment now.'

From down below several men muttered comments that were too low for him to hear, but the lack of further gunfire suggested that no duplicity had taken place during the surrender.

Along the length of the hollow Houston's men stared at the point where the slope became steeper and kept Brady and his men hidden, waiting with their guns aimed forward for the first man to risk coming closer. But when one man did appear, he only darted up for a moment before going back to ground. Even so several bullets whined over his form.

Then from the man's position a flaming object hurtled into the night sky. He had aimed it well and the object went unerringly on a direction that would land it in the middle of the hollow. It turned end over end, the air rushing by flaring its form and making it difficult to identify.

Then Dalton saw what it was and winced.

'Dynamite,' he muttered, then shouted for everyone to hear. 'It's dynamite. Run!'

Nobody needed another warning. As the dynamite slammed to the ground in a shower of sparks, everyone scattered.

With Dalton and Loren being at the right of the hollow they ran that way while the others ran in the opposite direction. They'd been running for only a few seconds when the explosion ripped out, knocking Dalton to his knees then flat forward.

As he lay on his chest with his hands raised to protect his head, grit and pebbles peppered his back. When the blast had receded, he glanced at Loren, who gave him a brief smile to confirm he was fine. Then he looked back to see that they'd covered around thirty yards and that they were away from the main blast area.

Beyond the spreading ball of smoke he could hear Houston shouting for his men to get down, so he judged that most of the group had escaped the explosion. Then the smoke spread out to engulf Dalton and Loren as, from down the hill, Brady issued orders to surround them.

'Soon as the smoke clears,' Loren murmured, 'we don't stand a chance out here in the open.'

'Agreed,' Dalton said, 'we need to get moving.'

Loren nodded. They set off along the top of the hill, using their memory of the journey from the cave to the pit yesterday.

The smoke continued to expand, masking their progress. By the time they could see for some distance, they had reached lower ground and were standing between the cave and the entrance to the mine encampment.

On one side Cornelius was lying dead. On the other side Brady's men were swarming over the hill, keeping their profiles low as they closed on the hollow. Dalton couldn't see where Houston had gone to ground but he was heartened to note that nobody was looking their way.

'There's a good chance Brady will wipe out Houston,' Loren said, 'but unless we get help there's no chance of us doing the same to Brady.'

'Except one,' Dalton said. He drew Loren's

attention to the tents where around a dozen miners had emerged to watch proceedings, while staying far enough away to avoid getting caught up in the crossfire.

'The mine's being fought over. It has nothing to do with them.'

'It has everything to do with them and if I've judged those men correctly, they still have pride in themselves.'

Loren gave Dalton a narrowed-eyed look that said his record recently as regards understanding people's motivations had been poor. But Dalton still hoped Owen wouldn't disappoint him. He pointed out the route they'd need to take to reach the encampment.

'All right,' Loren said. 'But only because being over there is safer than being over here.'

With that comment they ran down the rest of the slope. They'd reached the bottom when Brady and Houston's groups started trading gunfire. Both men looked back to confirm that no attention was being paid to them. Then they put that stand-off from their minds and ran for the encampment.

They'd covered half the distance before anyone paid them any attention. Then the miners grouped together with one man stepping forward, and Dalton wasn't surprised to see that man was Sheckley.

'That's far enough,' Sheckley shouted, raising a warning hand.

They kept running until they reached the tents, the miners eyeing their every pace with suspicion.

Then, on Sheckley's orders, they formed a loose circle around them.

'We need your help,' Dalton said.

His request received a chorus of snorts.

'Why? Are you planning to steal more clothes or use the Durando women first again?'

'Nothing like that. As I tried to tell you back in Durando, we're friends of Perry Haynes. We aim to restore him as the mine owner and then life will be better for everyone.'

Sheckley pointed at the gun battle now raging on the hill.

'And that's making it better?'

'It will, if you join me in taking on Brady and Houston.'

Sheckley spread his hands. 'Cornelius never allowed anyone but his own men to bring guns into the mine. Anyone who goes over there will get slaughtered.'

Dalton noted that he hadn't received an outright refusal and he backed away a pace. He looked at the hill as he chose his next words carefully.

'Then do nothing and be downtrodden all your life, but if I were you I'd been more interested in those dead men with guns over there.'

This comment made several miners look at the bodies by the mine entrance. The first inkling that they'd join Dalton lit their eyes, but they still looked to Sheckley for his approval, and he was shaking his head as he paced towards Dalton.

'There's no point,' he said as reached out to grab

Dalton's collar and drag him up close. 'Nobody has seen Perry Haynes for months. He's dead, and so will you be after I've finished off what I started yesterday.'

Dalton kept his hands by his side and raised his chin.

'Perry is still alive.' Dalton grunted when Sheckley tightened his grip of his collar. 'What will it take to convince you?'

'Show us Perry and I'll believe you,' Sheckley snarled.

'I don't know where he is.'

Sheckley sneered and drew back his fist. Then a miner murmured something and he glanced over his shoulder. A slow smile spread over his face. He threw Dalton away from him and set his hands on his hips.

'Then maybe you ain't as clever as you reckon you are, because I know exactly where he is.'

'Where?' Dalton murmured. Loren nudged him in the ribs and pointed.

He turned, to see a wagon coming into the mine. He narrowed his eyes and saw that Owen Muldoon was riding up front with Mattie. Between them rode the smiling figure of Perry Haynes.

'It appears I was wrong,' Loren said, watching the wagon head towards them, a slow smile spreading. 'Owen's brought Mattie.'

'I always knew he'd come.' Dalton paced away from the tents towards the approaching wagon. He avoided meeting Loren's eyes to ensure he wouldn't see how much he'd doubted it himself.

'Appears to be some trouble over there,' Owen

said. He drew the wagon to a halt and looked at the hill, from where rapid gunfire was blasting out.

'Which has nothing to do with you, seeing as how it's happening outside Durando.'

'Just what I thought,' Owen said, his voice light as he joined in the good-humoured jesting. 'But while I was out this way admiring the view, I collected someone who wanted to see you.'

He leaned back. Perry worked his way along the seat, jumped down from the wagon and joined Dalton and Loren.

'I'd hoped you'd heard us back in the tunnel,' Dalton said.

'Sure did,' Perry said. 'Got to admit at first I wondered what you were doing, but I gave you the benefit of the doubt. I'm pleased to see I was right and I'm grateful for what you've done.'

Perry looked up at Mattie and smiled.

'Seeing you daughter in a safe place,' Loren said, 'and you outside that prison is all we ever needed to see.'

'I know.' Perry swung round to look at the hill. 'So what's your plan for the rest?'

Dalton stood beside him. 'To be honest it wasn't much of a plan other than to set everyone off against their rivals. But it's worked so far. Cornelius is dead and Brady and Houston are busy deciding who'll take his place.'

'Except they won't, with your help.'

'Not just mine.' Dalton backed away to let Perry see the gathered miners behind him. 'I reckon they all want this to end the right way too.'

Perry firmed his jaw. He looked at the cluster of miners, then paced over to them. He set his feet wide apart and spoke in an authoritative way that Dalton hadn't heard from him before.

'I ran the mine fairly and paid a good wage to any man who was prepared to do an honest day's work. With your help those days can return.'

A subdued and ragged cheer went up. When that approval dragged a few more miners out of their tents Perry's words got passed from man to man. Then enthusiastic murmuring started, followed by a heartier cheer that was loud enough to be heard over on the hill.

Dalton caught Sheckley's eye and received a nod. Then everyone turned to look at the hill.

The smoke had cleared and Brady had lit a line of brands, letting it be seen that Houston was making a stand around fifty yards from the hollow, behind a low tangle of boulders. As there was little cover available Brady was being cautious in approaching him and neither side was making much leeway.

'This ain't going to be easy,' Dalton said. He looked at Perry, who was still patting the miners who had agreed to help him on the back. Then he looked at Owen, who smiled.

'It seems to me,' Owen said, hitching his gun belt higher, 'that you need the help of a man who might one day be the marshal of Durando.'

'I do,' Dalton said. 'Even when that marshal isn't in Durando.'

Owen nodded. He drew his gun. 'When I'm not in town, I tend to use a simple plan.'

He set off walking towards the hill.

'Which is?' Dalton called after him.

'Get 'em!' Owen roared, breaking into a run.

CHAPTER 13

Bemused, Dalton watched Owen run towards the hill. His sudden movement and rallying call was the very spur the miners needed to push them into action. Around twenty men hurried after Owen, eager now to be among the first to reach the hill and so claim a gun.

Dalton and Loren followed him at a more leisurely place. Perry stayed back a moment or two, to instruct Mattie to stay by the tents. Then he too hurried after them.

From the way Owen had acted Dalton couldn't help but think he had been waiting for this opportunity to act all along. Either way he had been right to trust him, but as they closed on the hill he put that from his mind and concentrated on the struggle ahead.

The men on the hill hadn't registered that they were being approached, each group being too involved in their own battle for supremacy. So when the slope took them out of view Owen tried to maintain the element of surprise. After the miners had collected the spare guns, he gathered them to him. He put a finger to his lips, then beckoned for them to spread out along the base of the hill and to stay crouched down.

Dalton and Loren took up a position at the end of the line, while Owen and Perry took up the opposing flanking position. Then they set off up the slope.

Slowly the top of hill appeared ahead and when they were level with the hollow Dalton saw that the situation was becoming difficult for Houston. Several of his hired guns were lying sprawled over his covering boulders.

This success had emboldened Brady. His men were creeping closer on all fours, aiming to come at Houston's position from several directions. But, unseen by them, forty yards down the slope the miners were advancing and aiming to use the same tactic against them.

One careful pace at a time both groups closed on their targets, each man creeping along the ground while keeping his gaze set forward. Dalton judged that this situation couldn't last for long. And he was right.

Ten yards to his side a miner dislodged a stone, which rattled down the slope. Then the man stumbled. The noise was loud enough to make one of Brady's men look backwards. He was confronted with the sight of a line of men creeping up on them. He cried out, making his associates swirl round and

Houston and his two surviving men bob up.

For a long moment all three groups looked at each other. Then they all fired at once.

Dalton dived forward to present as low a profile as possible. He picked off a man trailing at his end of the line. The miners all fired at the man nearest to them. So, trapped between Houston's men and the advancing miners, Brady's men fared badly.

Dalton counted five men going down in the first onslaught before the rest dived to the ground. Even then, with gunfire raging from Houston's position and from further down the slope, another two men cried out then went rolling away.

This was too much for the rest. As one they took flight. Whether they went in search of better cover or ran in sheer self-preservation Dalton couldn't tell, but Houston and the miners made them pay.

Rapid gunfire made several of the fleeing men go tumbling down. In the midst of the rout Brady ran one way then another, unsure upon which group he should take out his anger. As Houston stood and fired at his men he made his decision and the two rivals faced each other.

Over twenty yards of barren ground they squared up to each other. Then they both fired. Houston fired wildly and he paid for his poor aim when he stumbled, clutching his wounded shoulder before Brady's second shot sent him spinning out of sight.

Brady then took stock of the situation. Seeing his men fleeing in all directions and hearing Owen and Perry shouting for the miners to take him, he took flight too. But he ran off in the opposite direction to most of his men, with only two men accompanying him, and headed straight for Dalton and Loren's position.

'Get ready,' Loren urged Dalton.

Dalton nodded. The two men settled down and awaited Brady. They watched him run past, keeping his head down as he hurried away from the main fighting.

'Now,' Dalton said and fired.

Loren joined him in shooting a moment later, but as they fired one of the men ran in front of Brady. This man went down, holed in the chest, making Brady swing round and return fire that made Dalton and Loren lie flat. His shots clattered into rock beside them.

They looked up to see Brady come to a sudden halt, wheeling his arms as he fought for balance.

Dalton craned his neck to see what the problem was. He saw that Brady had halted on the edge of the hollow. Presumably the explosion had widened the hole and Brady was trying to avoid falling.

As several miners peppered gunfire at Brady, he righted himself, then ran over to one of the brands he'd brought up to light up the hill. The other man with him collapsed, shot in the back, but Brady ignored him. He threw the brand into the hollow then followed it down and moved out of sight.

'Escaped,' Loren muttered, loosing off a shot in irritation.

'Not for long,' Dalton said. 'He won't know the

terrain down there and even if he gets lucky, we can block off his escape routes.'

'That's assuming a lot, and either way, he don't deserve to be safe when the rest of his men are fighting for their lives.'

'Agreed,' Dalton said. He looked up and saw that even without their leader Brady's men had retreated behind Houston's cover and were now fighting back against the miners. 'You help them. I'll get Brady.'

Loren shook his head. 'We'll get him together.'

'We won't. I'm the one who knows the tunnels down there, not you.'

Loren firmed his jaw, looking as if he'd argue, then nodded.

'All right,' he said, 'I'll cover you.'

He swung round and laid down gunfire at the boulders. Wasting no time, Dalton got to his feet and with his head down he ran to the hollow. The hole opened up before him, confirming that the explosion had ripped a wide hole in the ground.

As he approached, more of the inside appeared as the brand that Brady had thrown lit up the now wide hole. Brady was nowhere to be seen.

Dalton reached the edge and peered down, confirming that Brady wasn't visible, then he looked for the safest way down.

A hand grabbed his ankle and yanked, tumbling him down on to his side.

He just had time to realize that Brady hadn't gone down into the hole, but instead had skirted around

145

the edge before Brady swung his gun around towards him.

Lying on his side Dalton threw out an arm. With the back of his hand he slapped Brady's shoulder. The blow landed without much force but it was enough to make the gun veer away from him.

Then he threw himself at Brady. He wrapped both arms around the man's chest and knocked him backwards. The blow jarred the gun away.

Then both men went tumbling. Entangled, they rolled once before the ground collapsed beneath them. They both dropped into the hole.

They rushed through the air. Then they slammed to the ground. The debris cushioned Dalton's fall, but he still rolled to the side away from Brady, winded.

He lay for a moment gathering his breath, then staggered to his feet. Disorientated he lurched away. He reached for his holster to find that his own gun had been shaken free. He swung round to see that Brady had sat up and was looking at him, shaking his head to gather his senses.

Then Brady's eyes lit upon Dalton's gun. It was lying two feet in front of him and ten feet away from Dalton.

'Unarmed and helpless,' Brady said, grinning eagerly. He made a move for the gun.

Dalton jerked forward, aiming to make a grab for the weapon, but before he'd managed even a single pace Brady had slapped a hand on it.

Dalton stopped himself, cast a quick glance

around the top of the hole. He saw that he would receive no help. He turned on his heel and ran for the tunnel through which they'd entered the area earlier.

On the run he scooped up the brand that Brady had thrown into the pit, then he slipped into the tunnel. A bullet kicked rock slithers away from the entrance; the shards sliced at his back.

He ran down the tunnel. It was narrow and had a curve that was sharp enough to take him out of sight after about ten yards, so he scurried on with his head down.

He heard Brady edge into the tunnel behind him and fire. The bullet whined and clattered down the tunnel, scything past his shoulder before ricocheting along. Dalton gritted his teeth and ran on when he could, negotiating other areas sideways when they narrowed.

Another slug whined past his shoulder, tearing pebbles from the roof. He moved around the curve for far enough to avoid a direct shot. Brady still tore off another wild shot before he concentrated on running after him.

Dalton reached the opening to the tunnel where it emerged into a large cave. He turned to the side to enter the next tunnel.

A thud, followed by a curse sounded as Dalton cut off the light in the tunnel behind him, making Brady's progress harder. Dalton smiled to himself. He decided that in this case having light was probably preferable to having a gun. He ran on to the tunnel that led out of the cave, where he glanced back to see that Brady still hadn't emerged.

He concentrated on running and putting as much distance as he could between himself and Brady.

'Dalton!' Brady shouted behind him, his voice echoing in the confined space. 'You won't escape. I can see you.'

Dalton reckoned he could only see the light, so he carried on. The tunnel he was in was straight and ahead was the thin rock seam that he would have to slip through before he reached another cave. After that there was another tunnel and then the pit where he would be trapped if the ropes they'd climbed down were no longer there.

Dalton made a sudden decision. When he reached the seam he did a sharp turn to the right and ran down the tunnel he'd explored in error earlier that night. This movement cut off the light in the other tunnel instantly and Dalton was rewarded when Brady cursed again.

He kept running until he reached the cave that contained numerous holes. He slipped into a recess beside the entrance where he placed the brand against the wall and shielded it to limit the light that would filter out.

He hoped that Brady would now have no light to guide him, that he would eventually find the rock seam, then work his way through it and become hopelessly lost.

This appeared to be what had happened when from some distance away he heard a thud, presumably as Brady walked into a wall. A prolonged bout of cursing was followed by the sounds of Brady scrabbling at the walls.

Then footfalls sounded, coming closer.

Dalton winced, accepting that more light from the brand must be filtering out than he had hoped. So he swung out of the recess to look around the cave.

He had explored only a few of the other holes earlier. Entering any of them could get him lost within minutes or, worse, trap him in a dead end, but he figured he didn't have a choice.

He chose a tunnel that was straight ahead and which he could see went on for a while, but by the time he reached it Brady's footfalls were already closing.

He ran on, the brand held high, his quick motion flaring the light. It illuminated the way ahead, showing him that twenty yards on the tunnel closed then veered downwards and to the left.

'Nowhere to hide, Dalton,' Brady taunted him, his voice sounding near enough to make Dalton look back.

He saw Brady standing in the tunnel entrance, his gun drawn and an arm held out to show that Dalton couldn't get past him.

Dalton ignored the taunt. He carried on to the corner where he saw that the tunnel headed down into a cave, about ten feet across. He ran into it, looked around for a way out, then gulped.

There was no way out.

He skidded to a halt. He held the brand up to

illuminate every darkened cranny of the small cave, but it was enclosed. The only way out was the way he'd come in, a way that the armed Brady now blocked.

Dalton fought down the panic that tightened his throat. He looked around again. This time he saw a small boulder lying on a slightly raised patch of loose pebbles, which he hadn't seen before.

He raised the brand but the improved light couldn't remove the shadow behind the boulder.

Dalton ran for the area, hoping the shadow would turn out to be a hole, but when he clambered up the pebbled slope and lit the area, only the cave wall was there.

He was trapped.

He swirled round to see Brady pace into the cave entrance. Brady glanced around, taking in the surroundings and nodding to himself.

'Kill me,' Dalton said, 'and you kill yourself.'

'I ain't a fool,' Brady said. 'The miners say you can get lost under here, but they exaggerated. I remembered the way I came in. I can easily get out.'

Brady raised his gun to aim at Dalton's chest. He was smiling.

'I'm sure you can get out when you can see where you're going.' Dalton raised the brand then dashed it to the pebbles at his feet. 'But what about in the dark?'

The light flared through the air then spluttered on the ground, Dalton's hopes that the light would extinguish immediately were not realized, but the light level dropped enough to stay Brady's hand.

'Don't!' he shouted, stepping forward.

Heartened, Dalton kicked out. He scooped up the brand along with a heap of pebbles and launched them at Brady. The brand flew wide of its target and hit the wall, then dropped to the ground, but the pebbles dashed against Brady's chest making him flinch away.

He straightened up, but it was to face Dalton, who threw himself from the slope. With his arms thrust forward Dalton slammed into him.

Both men went down heavily with Dalton on top, grabbing for the gun. To their side the brand sputtered, throwing up huge shadows of the two men as they struggled for supremacy.

They rolled from side to side. Both men got a hand on the gun and squeezed out a shot that whirred and pinged off the walls around them.

Then it all went dark.

Dalton couldn't help but look at the brand, but saw only after-images of its previous light. Even if he could get to it he judged that it was already dead. He put the brand and the gun from his mind and thought of his only advantage.

He thumped Brady in his stomach, then rolled off his chest and moved to get away. Brady grabbed a trailing leg. Dalton kicked his hand away and ran off into the darkness. He thrust his hands out to touch the walls and that helped him to orient himself and run on at almost the pace he had managed in the light.

'Dalton!' Brady shouted, but got no reply as Dalton gave him no clues as to his exact whereabouts.

A gunshot sounded, then a second, but they were fired from some distance behind him and the ricochets came nowhere near him. His footfalls then echoed back at him and he judged he'd reached the main cave.

He took a few more paces then stretched out a hand. He found the tunnel he would have to go down to reach the rock seam, after which, if his good judgement held, he could reach the surface. But Brady in the darkness would need more than just that knowledge.

Dalton stopped and turned.

'I'm here,' he shouted. His voice echoed. He hoped it would give Brady no clues as to where he actually was. 'The miners were right. Men with torches could die down here trying to find a way out and you ain't got a light.'

'I'll get you, Dalton,' Brady shouted, his voice sounding some distance away.

'You won't. You might find your way out, but we'll be waiting for you. And if you don't come out, nobody will ever come in to find you.'

'I'll shoot you to hell!' A gunshot tore out, then another.

'Save your bullets, Brady.' Dalton forced a mocking burst of laughter. 'Or at least save one bullet.'

Then he turned on his heel and with his arms

outstretched he headed off into the dark, hoping he wouldn't be doomed to roam the tunnels until he came to envy Brady for having a gun.

CHAPTER 14

After an increasingly worrying forty minutes of slow progress, Dalton found his way out of the underground passages, emerging outside the mine. Twice he'd gone down wrong tunnels but each time he'd kept his rising panic at bay and had retraced his steps until he'd found the right way.

Of Brady he had heard nothing.

The ropes down into the hole were still there, so he climbed out easily. When he rolled on to the surface it was to face the welcoming sight of the advancing Loren.

'Brady?' Loren asked.

'He and Cornelius let plenty of men die underground as punishment. I reckon he's now regretting that, but if he finds his way out, he can have a more traditional punishment.'

Loren agreed with this. They returned to the mine to find that the situation was now under control. The bloodbath that Dalton had feared hadn't come about, as after Brady had fallen into the hole the rest of his men had given themselves up and were now being held prisoner.

Perry was debating with the miners what he should do with them. As neither Dalton nor Loren reckoned this was a matter for them to worry about they joined Owen.

'You not dealing with the prisoners?' Dalton asked.

'Nope,' Owen said. 'As I told you, I look after the law in Durando. What happens elsewhere is no concern of mine.'

Dalton smiled on noting Owen had referred to the law and not to his doing what he was paid to do.

'Yeah. I saw how unconcerned you were.'

Owen winked then tipped his hat. They stood in companionable silence until Perry came over to join them.

'We're leaving,' Loren said. 'We reckon we've spent enough time here.'

'I thought you'd head back to Two Forks,' Perry said, smiling, 'but remember that you're always welcome here.'

'We're obliged for that,' Dalton said, 'but don't take it the wrong way when we say that even with you and Owen being in charge, neither of us will be in a hurry to come here again.'

'I understand, but you should return to see the good you've done in making Durando a safer place.' Perry glanced at his daughter. 'For all of us.'

Loren followed his gaze then coughed and leaned forward.

'You thought that once before, so if you ever doubt it again, remember that Two Forks is a safe place for someone as precious as Mattie.'

Mattie considered Loren with her head cocked on one side, as did Dalton. Slowly a smile spread.

'I reckon,' she said, 'I'd appreciate seeing a town that's a mite more appealing than Durando.'

Loren returned her smile. Leaving them to settle down to discuss the details Dalton went to find his horse.

Thirty minutes later he'd found it, along with Loren's wagon. So after riding past Owen and receiving a farewell nod he collected Loren.

At a steady pace they headed out of the mine.

'When is she coming to Two Forks?' Dalton asked as they trundled down into the pass.

'Soon, I hope,' Loren said. He looked ahead at the horizon, where the first hints of daybreak were lighting the summer sky. 'I'm coming back here in a few weeks. What happens then will be up to her.'

This news sounded good to Dalton. With a smile he moved to hurry his horse on, but then a twinkling light to his side caught his attention. He drew his horse to a halt and looked down, frowned, then dismounted to explore further.

The twinkle came again and he saw that it came from a rock that was catching a stray beam of light. On closer examination it appeared that a pebble-sized nugget of gold was trapped in a larger rock. He hefted it then got back on his horse.

'Gold,' he said, 'possibly from Kyle's wagon when

he was escaping.'

'It'll make a nice present for Eliza after being away for longer than you promised.'

'I gave her that nugget I found last year.' Dalton tossed the rock to Loren. 'You keep it and make it into something nice for Mattie.'

Loren considered the small golden pebble. 'For Mattie? So you reckon the daughter of a man who owns a gold mine will be impressed by this?'

'Not the gold, but the man giving it to her.'

Loren smiled at that but he still tossed it back to Dalton.

'I hope she will, but I've had enough of gold.'

Dalton nodded and looked around. In the growing light he saw other twinkling objects. They could be gold nuggets or maybe they were false sightings of shiny rocks.

He was curious enough to look out for more. Then, with a shiver, he tossed the pebble over his shoulder.

'Me too,' he said as it clattered to the ground. 'Where we're going we ain't got no use for it.'

Loren's smile said that he agreed. The two friends galloped away from the mine, eager now to reach Two Forks and normality as quickly as possible.